THE QUEST
OF THE THOUGHT
TRAVELLERS

S.E.STEWART

 FriesenPress

Suite 300 - 990 Fort St
Victoria, BC, V8V 3K2
Canada

www.friesenpress.com

Copyright © 2017 by S.E.STEWART
First Edition — 2017

Editing by Sara Deabler and Gary Garrison

ISBN
978-1-4602-9889-3 (Hardcover)
978-1-4602-9890-9 (Paperback)
978-1-4602-9891-6 (eBook)

1. JUVENILE FICTION, FANTASY & MAGIC

Distributed to the trade by The Ingram Book Company

Dedicated to Sorcha, Evan, and Adrian

TABLE OF CONTENTS

PROLOGUE
MERLIN'S PROPHECY

Three shall return from out the West
To put the evil spells to rest:
The Singer as in legend told,
The Warrior with a temper bold,
The Sage with knowledge new and old.
Their return begins the quest
To wake the wizard from his rest
And drive the darkness back.

At her throat she wears the stone.
She sings her song. It's hers alone.
Song and stone unknit the night,
Unwind the colours true and bright,
Unmake the one that Merlin made,
And make the light come back again
To crack the rock, complete the age,
To free the Thought and free the Mage
And drive the darkness back.

CHAPTER ONE
THE STONE

"Out you go! AND STAY OUT!" Aunt Maer shooed the three children out of the house. "I am so tired of you tramping in mud all over my clean floors! And if you go in the woods, stay on the path! And don't you dare go near that waterfall, Rory. It's too dangerous."

"She is such a pain, going on all the time about being clean, being tidy, being quiet. I wish we had never come to stupid Wales for the summer. I wish I was back in Toronto," complained Rory, kicking stones as he walked.

"Quit whining," sighed his sister Mackenzie. "It's not like we had a choice." Tom, their younger brother, ignored it all. He had his nose stuck in his bird watchers' notebook and was jotting down the birds he spotted.

The path in the woods was muddy after the rain in the night, but the sun was now shining, and the trees were full of birdsong. Mackenzie began humming a tune, which steadily grew into a sweet melody. These songs often just popped into her head, but she never shared them. She doubted that anyone would ever want to listen to her anyway. When she auditioned for the school choir, she didn't even get chosen. Miss Fracknell, the choir teacher, told her she was a rusty nail, a little phrase she used to label the worst singers.

"Shut *up* Mackenzie!" shouted Rory. "I'm so sick of your screeching!"

Mackenzie ignored him and, to drown his complaints, rapped out, *"Rory is my brother, and he's not cool. He's the biggest bully in Glenview School."*

Some stones landed in the leaves in front of her. The next ones were better aimed.

"Ouch!" cried Mackenzie. "Stop kicking those stones, Rory. That one hurt. It got me on the leg."

"It wasn't my fault. You were in the way. Ugh, I just want to do something—exciting!"

"Like what?" asked Mackenzie.

"Let's explore a bit. We could go down to that waterfall! You know, the one they call Witch's Cauldron? Or we could go up that big hill and climb the stone circle at the top."

"No way," said Tom. "It's too hot to climb. And anyway, we can't go to the waterfall. You heard what Aunty Maer said."

"You heard what Aunty Maer said," mimicked Rory. "You are such a little goody-goody. It's bad enough being dumped in the middle of nowhere for a month, but it's worse still being dumped here with you. If you're not bird watching, you're star gazing or reading the dictionary and acting like you know it all."

"Better than being a know-nothing like you," Tom squeaked.

Mackenzie stalked ahead, ignoring them. She was sick of them always fighting, usually about nothing at all. They were used to the distractions of Toronto with all their friends, canoeing on the lakes in Northern Ontario and going camping. Here they were, without Mom and Dad and no friends. Just each other.

"Why did we have to come to Wales of all places?" she muttered to herself. "All because Mom was brought up here by Grandma's sister, Aunt Maer. I wish I could have stayed with—"

Suddenly she heard Tom swearing and turned to see Rory shove him hard. Tom grabbed Rory's legs and pulled him down. They rolled on the ground and were soon filthy with mud.

"Break it up, you two!" Mackenzie hauled Tom to his feet, wondering how she could distract them. She spotted a derelict cottage not far off and got an idea.

"How about we take a look at that cottage? We could probably explore inside. It looks like no one lives there."

"Yeah!" Rory was excited. "What if it's a robbers' hideaway?"

Tom bristled. "We're not supposed to . . ."

"Do anything fun?" Rory finished for him. "Yes, I know."

"We'll come right back to the path after," Mackenzie reassured Tom, who shrugged and walked behind his siblings.

As they got nearer, they saw that the cottage was badly neglected. It was built of crumbling stone covered with creeper. The garden was overgrown with stinging nettles and bindweed that gave off a dank, sour smell.

"I dare someone to knock on the door," whispered Rory.

"It's not much of a dare," scoffed Mackenzie. "It's obvious no one lives there. It's just a ruin."

"No, it's not," huffed Tom, catching up to them. "Listen!" Very faintly they could hear the sound of clucking. "See? They keep hens."

"Just makes it more exciting, doesn't it?" said Rory. "Someone could come at any minute! Don't be a chicken, chicken!"

Tom looked worried.

Rory smirked at his brother.

"Are you accepting the dare, then?"

"Let's figure out who has to knock," Mackenzie said quickly. "We'll use my necklace for choosing, like I do at school."

"Even though you're not allowed," mumbled Tom.

Mackenzie undid the catch from around her neck and held up her necklace between them. They all knew how to play. The single crystal swung on the chain as all three held out their right hands. It caught the sunlight as it swung, forming a rainbow of colours that dyed their faces for just a moment, first red, then blue, then violet.

Whichever hand the stone swung toward was the chosen one. After circling clockwise for a bit, the stone started to swing towards Mackenzie's hand and back to the center.

"It's you!" laughed Rory.

"No, just wait a minute. It might change," she hesitated. The stone continued to go towards her. With a sinking heart, she realized she would have to take Rory's dare.

"I'm glad it's not me." Tom was relieved.

"You're such a baby," whispered Rory.

"You guys will wait for me while I do it, right?"

They nodded, then hid behind some gooseberry bushes.

Mackenzie walked slowly up the overgrown path. It was unnaturally quiet.

"I'm not really scared," she thought to herself. "There's probably nobody here, and anyway, I'm a fast runner."

The door was overgrown with convolvulus. Beneath the creeper the green paint was flaking off the ancient door. The knocker was a rusty ball on a chain. She let it swing against the door where it made a dent and chipped more of the paint. There was silence; then suddenly Mackenzie heard footsteps and a cough. The doorknob turned. Mackenzie swung on her heel and took off down the path, but she was not fast enough. Someone grabbed her arm, and she was dragged inside, screaming. The door locked behind her. It was too dark to make out who her captor might be, but she could tell he was about the same size she was, only much stronger. Try as she might, she could not wriggle free.

"I will not harm thee, Mistress!" shouted the figure. "Hush, hush! It is me, Esti." Mackenzie continued screaming, and eventually he let go.

"Hold thy whist, Mistress!" he whispered.

Released, Mackenzie quieted. She needed to keep her strength and her wits about her.

"It is only me Mistress," came the reply in a rough but respectful voice. "I am Esti. Don't you know me? We must be quick, for Vivienne will soon return!"

Mackenzie got control of her ragged breathing. "Why did you grab me? You really scared me!"

"I did not mean to alarm you. Pray, come out to the garden. This house is so full of enchantments. I cannot trust even the spiders spinning in their webs."

Mackenzie shuddered as she felt something sticky brush against her cheek.

She followed Esti running through the dark passage, which ran from the front to the back door. With relief, she was out in the sunshine.

Mackenzie could now see that Esti was just a small boy. He was very unkempt and very ugly. His body was hunched over as if worn out by long hours of backbreaking work. He wore a short woollen cloak of olive green with the hood pulled back and fastened with a long rusty pin. His shirt was torn and filthy and tucked into coarse brown sacking pants. There were no shoes on his feet, which were so misshapen she thought that probably none would fit.

Esti stared at her through his thick, matted hair, which looked as if it had never seen a comb, never mind a bottle of shampoo! How strange his face is, she thought. He looked both young and old at the same time. And his eyes! They are bright green, like summer leaves.

Esti reached for her hands and held them in his. "I saw you outside. You are the guardian of the stone! I know 'tis you."

Mackenzie felt her heart thump against her ribs. "What do you know about my stone?" She pulled her hands away and cradled her stone, sheltering it from his gaze. The crystal dazzled like iced fire through her fingers.

"I know this stone of old, and I have been waiting for you, the keeper of the stone."

"What are you talking about?"

"Why do you pretend you do not understand me?" He choked back a sob. "I thought it meant you had come to rescue me."

Mackenzie, thinking the boy crazy but harmless, reached out and patted his shoulder gently. He obviously had not lived in the real world much. And the way he talked was very odd and quite old fashioned. She was sorry he seemed so upset.

"Get your hands off her! Leave her alone!" Rory crashed around the side of the house, Tom following some distance behind. Rory grabbed Esti and threw him to the ground, sitting across the boy's chest and threatening him with a fist.

"Leave my sister alone!"

"I didn't mean no harm. Let me go! I would never hurt her. She's the one who keeps the stone!" To their horror Esti began to weep, making sounds like a little animal in pain. Rory scrambled up, but the boy continued to lie on the ground, curled up and crying. His shirt had rucked up, and Mackenzie saw bruises all over his back, as though someone had been hurting him on purpose. She wondered if the boys noticed.

Mackenzie coaxed Esti to his feet, wiping his tears with the sleeve of her shirt and patting his shoulder gently.

"What's he talking about?" demanded Rory.

" It's about the stone on my necklace. I think he wants it—something to do with saving him. Please stop crying, Esti!" She could not stand to hear him sob like that.

"This is a special necklace," she said. "It's been in our family for years and years. It was my mother's and she gave it to me. I'm not really allowed to wear it. It has nothing to do with you, and it's not what you think it is! Please, *please* stop crying!"

Esti sucked in his tears. "I cease, mistress, when you tell me when we leave this cursed place." He smiled at them hopefully.

Rory shook his head. "We're not going anywhere. Not with you anyway."

The boy's face fell. "I don't understand. Why did you come? Are you tormenting me? Whose side are you on?" He eyed them suspiciously. "Did Vivienne send you?"

"We're not on anybody's side," said Rory.

"You must be on her side!"

"We're not on anybody's side, all right?" yelled Rory.

"Shut up Rory, you're not the boss," shouted Tom.

Esti was about to crumple again.

"Just leave him alone!" Mackenzie said. "Listen, Esti. *I'm* on your side. Tell me what's going on. Who's Vivienne?"

Esti looked around. "Wait, I must think. You have the stone. You knocked on my door. And yet. You do not know. I must trust you and tell . . ." Hoofbeats echoed through the woods. Someone was coming. Esti's eyes blazed with terror.

"Go! Go!" he screamed. "Vivienne's coming! I hear her. Quick! Hide the stone!"

Mackenzie slipped it down the front of her sweater.

"Meet me in the woods today, in the afternoon. I shall find you. Have no fear."

They turned to go but were not quick enough. A woman dressed in a red velvet riding habit galloped out of the wood beyond the garden. She was mounted on a black stallion. Horse and rider flew effortlessly over the stone garden wall and reined in beside them. The horse's ears flattened as the woman's harsh voice rang out.

"Get back into the house, Esti! How dare you disobey me!"

Esti trembled and scurried indoors. The woman stared down at the three children. Her face was icily beautiful.

"It was very kind of you to try and befriend Esti. I appreciate the kindness of strangers, but I must tell you, the boy is not well. Not well in his head, if you understand? He might even hurt you." She reached down and laid her long white hand on Mackenzie's shoulder and squeezed. Mackenzie winced. "Yes, he may be dangerous. You must keep away from him." Her smile was cold. "Stay away from Esti, or I think you might regret it."

CHAPTER TWO
THE ENCHANTRESS

"Look at the state of you!" cried Aunt Maer as they hurried into the kitchen. She was already serving lunch. Tom and Rory were still covered with mud. "Look at the pair of you! Rory, you're the oldest and should have more sense. What have you been doing?"

"Well," said Tom, "we met this boy in the wood. We were just being friendly, and this woman comes up and tells us off. We weren't doing anything either."

"Where was this?" Aunt Maer fixed them with a steely look.

"Nice going, big mouth," muttered Rory under his breath.

"Tom is a good boy for telling me. Now, where were you exactly?"

Tom stared down at his shoes.

"It was just by that old cottage place."

"The one off the path which I told you to stay on?"

The guilty looks on their faces told it all.

"What did I tell you? Stay on the path, I said!" she scolded. "You can get lost in those woods if you don't know your way. And as for that woman, she's a . . ." She raised her eyes to the ceiling but said no more.

"What's wrong with her?" asked Mackenzie, her curiosity thoroughly piqued.

Aunt Maer shook her head. "Go and wash your hands, and then we will have our lunch."

All three displayed their best table manners and said please and thank you so many times that Aunt Maer appeared to be in a better mood.

"Aunty Maer," began Mackenzie, "Who was that woman?"

"Ask no questions, and you'll hear no lies." Aunt Maer pulled her lips together and poured herself a cup of tea.

"What should we do if we see her again?" asked Tom, thoroughly rattled. "She was really scary."

None of the three mentioned Esti. They were in enough trouble.

"Listen, I'll tell you. But you must promise, on your honour, never to go down there again."

"Yes, we promise," said Mackenzie.

Aunt Maer whispered, "She's a witch."

There was a stunned silence, and then all three burst out laughing.

"I'm warning you," Aunt Maer said sternly. "It's not funny. Stay away from there. You don't want to worry your parents do you? Not at a time like this."

After lunch they were sent outside to shell peas. Tom remarked, when Aunt Maer was out of earshot, "Belief in witchcraft is still prevalent in some of these out-of-the-way country places in Europe."

"Stop showing off, Mr. Dictionary," said Rory. "She was just making that up. As if we were little kids."

"When we're done," Mackenzie announced, "I'm going back up to the woods to meet that boy, witch or no witch. I don't believe in them. So there! And I want to help him."

"Oh great!" snarled Rory. "He's a load of trouble. I didn't like him at all. Look at the way he was crying his eyes out about nothing!"

"And what if that Vivienne person was right? What if he's dangerous and meets us up there with a carving knife?" Tom squeaked. "Aunt Maer definitely wouldn't like it."

"I don't believe what that Vivienne woman said," insisted Mackenzie. "I want to know what Esti wants and what he knows about the stone in my necklace. It's really old, and it *is* from around here because great-grandmother had it when she was a girl and she grew up here."

"Yes, and Mom *also* said you weren't supposed to wear it until you were at least 16. You'll get it if she ever finds out!" Tom said.

"What's the point of having nice things if you can't wear them? You won't tell on me, will you, like you usually do?"

"Well, I can't tell Mom can I? Even if we were back home, I couldn't tell her." There was a catch in his voice that the other two pretended not to hear.

They sat in silence for a while.

"I don't care what you two think about it. I'm finished shelling the peas, and I'm going now." Mackenzie stood up to leave.

"Okay," said Rory. "I'll come too. I don't want to hang out here doing nothing. Come on, Tom."

"I'm staying here."

"Aunt Maer will only find you jobs to do if you're hanging around the house," warned Mackenzie. "Bring your bird book."

That seemed to convince him.

"Don't be scared. If he tries anything . . ." Rory clenched his fist and threw a punch at the air. "He'll have me to deal with."

Mackenzie walked ahead, thinking. She did not want to tell the boys what she really felt. She was haunted by the way the boy cried. She remembered crying like that herself very recently, but she did not, at the moment, want to remember why.

They walked for what seemed a long time. The trees melted into darkness on either side of the path, and they could see no sign of the strange-looking boy.

"How are we ever supposed to find him here?' complained Rory. "We could be wandering around for hours."

Just then they heard a whistle. They stopped by an old oak tree and looked around. They could see no sign of anyone. "Could have been a bird," said Tom, "but I don't recognize that call."

With one mind they flopped down on the ground, hot and tired. The tree trunk was split about halfway up, probably by lightning, to judge from the charred and blackened wood. Yet the tree had clung to life, for the branches above were spread thick, and the leaves made a big green umbrella above their heads. Mackenzie loved the way the leaves made strange flickering patterns on their bodies, as if they were turning into woodland creatures!

"Wow! Look at that!" Tom reached for his bird-spotting notebook. "It's really rare! A golden finch!"

Mackenzie watched it dart among the branches. "Strange," she mused, "how the leaves seem to make all kinds of shapes. You would almost swear there was a face up there."

"It is a face!" she cried as the face broke into a grin, and the next thing, there was Esti's face hanging upside down in front of her.

"I'm here!" he announced, sounding happier than at their last meeting. His legs were tucked around a lower branch, and he swung himself up into an arc and somersaulted effortlessly into the air to land on his feet before them. "Follow me!" Without waiting for an answer, he darted behind the tree. Bursting with curiosity, they followed and were just in time to see his bare feet disappear up a long rope.

Ignoring Rory's shouts of, "Let me go first! " and "Don't take your eyes off him!" Mackenzie grabbed hold of the rope and hauled herself up after Esti's dirty feet. The rope was knotted every so often, making it easy to climb, and soon she was so high she could see across a wild, waving sea of treetops. The boys looked tiny down below.

Suddenly, two strong brown hands grabbed her and pulled her to stand up on a broad branch.

"Here's where we can talk. It will be long before she thinks of looking for us up here."

It was like being in a big green circus tent. There were places to sit on the broad branches, and it was delightful to be up so high and yet feel safe. Mackenzie could look right down the centre of the blackened trunk almost to the ground. Rory and Tom joined them.

"Dost know why I brought you here?" Esti asked. "Especially here?" He looked at them eagerly.

"Well, no."

"A lightning-struck tree?" he prompted. "You know . . ."

"No, we don't." Rory was irritated.

"Tell us," said Mackenzie hurriedly.

"Just a minute!" Tom interjected. "A lightning-struck tree is . . ."

"A lightning-struck tree," interrupted Esti, "is the bridge between all worlds! From here we can travel to other times and other places."

"Cute make-believe games," muttered Rory, keeping his eyes glued on Esti's every move. Tom sat well away from them all.

"We can leave if you brought the stone," Esti said, ignoring Rory. Esti could not have failed to hear him.

"Listen, we'd better get a few things sorted out. You're going to have to tell us more," Mackenzie told him straight.

"I will honour your request, but first, did you bring the stone?

"Yes," said Mackenzie.

Esti sighed with relief. "I will tell you all I know. First, the stone is here," Esti counted on his fingers. "And second, there are three of you."

"There were last time I counted," said Rory.

"From whence do you come?"

"We're from Canada," said Mackenzie.

"What is Canada?'

Rory tapped his finger to his head and looked meaningfully at Mackenzie.

"Canada's a country," she went on quickly. "It's far to the west of here."

Esti's face lit up. "Yes! Yes! It is as prophesied. You have the stone, you are three, and the last sign is that you journeyed hence from the faerie lands to the west, from the land of eternal youth, the Isles of the Blessed."

"Faeries!" laughed Rory. "I'm not a faerie. Canada's a country where *people* live."

Esti blushed. "I never went to school. I know little of your world. But no matter. All is true. This is the song that has kept hope aflame in my heart. Listen!" Then he began to sing in a soft and crackled voice.

Three shall return from out the West
To put the evil spells to rest:
The Singer as in legend told,
The Warrior with a temper bold,
The Sage with knowledge new and old.
Their return begins the quest
To wake the wizard from his rest
And drive the darkness back.

At her throat she wears the stone.
She sings her song. It's hers alone.
Song and stone unknit the night,
Unwind the colours true and bright,
Unmake the one that Merlin made,
And make the light come back again
To crack the rock, complete the age,
To free the Thought and free the Mage
And drive the darkness back.

They looked at each other, puzzled. "What are you talking about?" said Rory.

The smile on Esti's face died. "You don't understand?" His brow furrowed in concentration as he sized them up in turn. Through the leaves the sun speckled his face, and he squinted hard, studying each of them. "Who are they, these three? Are they the ones? Why did they not know all that had occurred or the deliverance they would bring? The oldest one, Rory, he is big and strong, his hands always curled in a fist, his brow furrowed as if afraid to show his feelings. Look how he would defend his sister when he was afraid for her in the wood. Then there is the youngest one, Tom, wearing those funny round pieces of glassy shields on his eyes or else he cannot see. He is so scared of all that is yet seems to know so much. And Mackenzie, so shy and gentle, giving kindness to me yet so unsure of herself.

"Methinks that they may be The Three," he decided, "But only the wise can see through glamour to the true nature of things."

He spoke aloud, "Your disguise is indeed perfect. Vivienne herself did not realize who you were! She thought you were three children. But I warrant that you *are* the Warrior, the Sage, and the Singer."

They all burst out laughing. "I wonder who's who?" laughed Mackenzie, then suddenly paused and grew serious. "What does it mean?"

"Let me begin by telling you who I am," Esti whispered. "I am no boy, nor am I a man. I am just a thought held in the mind of my master, Merlin, the great magician. I was born into the world, a thought with a form, to be his companion and his help. I was made of a dream, woven with mist, tied with the twine of a strong spell. Only a great magician can make a thought such as I take form, and only the deepest magic can undo me."

Tom drew closer. Rory smirked. Esti had a faraway look in his eyes, and his voice grew stronger. "My maker, my father Merlin, was a great master of magic and a shape-shifter. He could fly like a falcon across the sky if he willed. He had great knowledge of all the secret mysteries and the wisdom to use his powers well. The stories of old tell how he was always beside his lord, Arthur the King. With Merlin's help, Arthur fulfilled his destiny. After 12 terrible and bloody battles, Arthur won the kingdom and held it thereafter.

"So Merlin's work was done and he longed for rest. He had grown old, and his body was no more than a cage of bones that trapped his soul. He went to live like a hermit, hidden in the woods, far from life at court. But growing lonely in his solitude, he used magic to create me, a boy who would be like a son to him. He called me Esti. Merlin was never lonely now, for he always had me by his side. I took care of both our needs. I lit the fire against the winter chill and brought water from the well.

"My father was all-knowing. He could see the past and the future. He warned me that he was doomed to suffer a dreadful enchantment and that dark ages were coming. He told me not to fear and taught me the song that I sang for you, which prophesied a time of healing yet to come. The Three would come and free Merlin from his enchantment and overcome the darkness.

"And so this doom came upon Merlin through the magic of a great and powerful enchantress. Her name is Vivienne. Although she was already powerful, she was greedy for more and more magic. She schemed by foul means to steal Merlin's power.

"Vivienne's strange beauty belongs to all those who are half faerie and half mortal. She used her beauty and her spells to captivate Merlin and make him love her. What could I do but witness his destruction? Merlin loved Vivienne so much he allowed her to charm his magic away. As he became weak, she became strong. Deep in the enchanted wood of Broceliand she wrought her last spell against him. She imprisoned him inside a rock. She imprisoned him and took me to be her slave. Thus she brought the shadows forth and reigns supreme.

"With the passing of Merlin, the realm was torn with strife. The light kindled by Arthur was extinguished, and the Dark Ages engulfed our island kingdom. The Faerie Folk and the Ancient Powers were driven out of this world and sailed for the Islands in the West. They left hill and stone circle, holy well and greenwood tree. All left. All except one."

"Who was it?" squeaked Tom.

"Vivienne, of course," Mackenzie answered.

"You mean Aunt Maer was right?" Tom's eyes were as big as saucers.

"She was only telling us stories to make us be more careful in the woods. Grow up!" sneered Rory.

Tom ignored him. "So Esti, you believe that we three are supposed to—what? Free Merlin from the stone and rescue you from Vivienne? Bring light and healing to our world? But Esti, we don't know how to do any of that stuff? We're still at school!"

"The stone. The stone has the power to transport us across time and space to where we must go. Then you will know what to do."

"This is so stupid!" cried Rory. "This isn't real! Time travelling? What a load of . . ."

"Be quiet, Rory," Mackenzie and Tom chorused.

"*Vivienne is real.*" Esti was solemn. "Very real and very dangerous, though she is not entirely mortal."

"And are *you* real, Esti?" asked Rory scornfully.

"I am just a thought, made of Merlin's mind by his magic."

Mackenzie touched the boy's arm gently. "You feel pretty solid to me. For a thought."

In the distance, faint and far away, they could hear hoofbeats. Esti looked round uneasily.

"Vivienne held me like a prisoner for all the years that have passed. But I knew you would come one day."

"Esti! Esti!" came a voice carried on the wind. "I command you, come to me!"

"She's looking for me. Quick, we must go. Please help me!" Agony shone bright in his eyes.

"I'll do it," promised Mackenzie. "It's okay. If I can, I will. Just tell me what to do."

Vivienne's voice was carried on the wind, turning now into a scream of rage.

"It has to be all or nothing. Three go or none." Esti looked at Tom, then at Rory.

"I don't believe a word of this," said Rory, "but, yes, I'll play. There isn't much else to do around here. Maybe it'll be fun."

"Count me out," announced Tom. "I'm going home!"

"Shush! Listen." There were the sounds of hoofbeats on the path they had come along before. "Don't move," whispered Esti.

Horse and rider galloped past the tree, and they breathed a sigh of relief. A moment later, the hoofbeats began again, coming back in their direction.

"You'd better not go down there, unless you want her to catch you," Mackenzie warned Tom. "You'd better stay with us."

Tom sat rock-still with fright. "I suppose I'll have to,"

"Willingly? You'll come?" Esti pleaded.

"It doesn't feel that way," began Tom, but fell silent as he looked into Esti's eyes. "Alright. Yes, I'll come willingly."

Esti breathed a sigh of relief. "Hurry, then. It is time for us to go to Broceliand. When we reach the rock we shall set Merlin free. We shall wake the wizard."

CHAPTER THREE
THE DRAGON

Mackenzie held the stone on its chain and spun it as Esti told her.

"Look at it, and never stop," he commanded.

They stared, fascinated as the jewel spun with a kaleidoscope of colours that dazzled their senses. It was as if every colour in the world had been sucked into the spinning crystal, and they were living inside a black-and-white photograph.

They felt sleepy but not tired at all. Their eyes blurred, and their bodies relaxed, curling into the nooks and crannies of the branches of the oak tree, and yet their minds were alert and active. With a sigh from the wind, the tree embraced their bodies and hid them with curtains of leaves. And so they dreamed together, the same dream. In the dream, they ran through the woods so fast their feet did not touch the grass. The wind blew fiercely in their faces, whipping their hair back. Once out of the woods, their eyes were dazzled by the huge orange sun. It seemed so low and yet moved fast, like a ball rolled by a giant. Below them lay a body of water so still and clear that all the hills around were perfectly reflected in its depths. It was hard to tell where reality stopped and reflection began. The deep blue water was speckled with wooded islands. Esti stopped, and they gathered round.

"Our dream has begun. Our journey has begun." Esti pointed to a dark and mysterious island that seemed to slumber on the water. "Our quest begins there."

They ran down to the shore and stared across the expanse of water, cold and brown.

"How do we get across?" asked Rory.

Esti looked up into the empty sky and furrowed his brow. "I call the birds."

He broke into squawks and shrieks.

"Are you sick?" asked Mackenzie.

"Birds don't come when you call," explained Tom patiently. But Esti was not listening to him. He was staring at Mackenzie.

"Will you sing for the birds?" he begged.

"Please! No!" Rory put his hands over his ears.

"What?" Mackenzie gaped. "I can't sing! How am I supposed to call birds?"

As soon as Esti asked her to sing, she felt her throat close up, and no sound came out at all!

"Please, Mackenzie! Hurry up! We cannot delay. Starting our quest depends on you now," Esti pleaded.

Mackenzie was so rattled that she took a deep breath, and out came a note. It was a little squeaky, but she was relieved that it was loud. Another deep breath and another note. Strangely, the wind slapping the water into little wavelets seemed to keep time with her voice. She grew bolder and sang again and again, a song that just seemed to make itself up as she sang. But was it going to be good enough?

The three children and Esti heard a humming that grew louder and louder. A dark cloud blotted out the sun. It was no cloud! A flock of birds! As they flew closer, the children saw tiny wings shimmering in shades of purple, gold, green, and red. Their beating wings made a wind that lifted Mackenzie's black hair so it streamed behind her like a cloak. As if of one mind, the birds gathered above the lake and made a living bridge to the island.

Tom jumped up and down in excitement. "Do you realize there is just about every single species of bird flying in that formation? Where's my camera? I need my bird book!"

"No time. Follow me!" cried Esti, and grabbed Tom's hand to pull him up onto the bridge of birds.

"They're holding us up!" screamed Tom. "Is it safe?"

"You don't weigh anything, Tom. You're just a dream. Remember, in dreams, magic happens!"

"Don't be such a baby, Tom!" shouted Rory. "This is so fun!"

The three of them were way out across the lake, heading towards the island, before realizing that Mackenzie was not following them.

"What is it?"

"I'm scared we'll hurt them," she cried.

"Come!" cried Esti. "They will hold us. I swear an oath to you that the bridge will hold! Make haste, for they will not tarry long."

Already some of the smaller birds were flying back into the sky.

Rory ran back to the shore, leaping over holes left by the birds who had already flown away. He grabbed Mackenzie by the hand and pulled her after him.

Mackenzie's yelp of fright changed into a cry of wonder as she felt the warmth of the birds hold her up. Stepping carefully from wing to wing, she drank in their beauty. The wings were like a carpet of colour that constantly changed patterns. The only sound was the low whirring of hundreds of wings beating the air.

Rory and Mackenzie came safely to Esti and Tom on the other side, but when they turned to see the way they had come, the birds had already dispersed. The four of them were standing on a narrow shore of white sand below towering cliffs. High above they saw silvery white flecks, gulls gliding effortlessly on the wind currents.

Esti was already leading the way on a path that zigzagged up the cliff face. Ahead of them, opening onto the path, was the dark mouth of a cave. In single file they followed behind Esti, but a short distance from the cave's mouth, they stopped.

"Is there anything in the cave?" asked Rory, ready to peer in.

Mackenzie held her nose. "Phew! Smells like rotting meat! Do we really want to find out?"

"Sure do, before we get any closer," advised Rory. "And I know just how to do that." He grabbed a large piece of flint lying on the ground. Then, before anyone could stop him, he ran up to the mouth of the cave and threw the rock inside.

Immediately there was a blood-curdling yell, and they shouted in terror as a mass of claws, feathers, and hot breath rushed at them and sent them half-falling, half-scrambling down to the bottom of the cliff. Bruised and scraped, they looked up to see a monstrous creature watching them from the path above. Their retreat was effectively cut off by the sea. They were trapped. Then they saw, with relief, that the beast was tethered by several feet of thick, golden chain. This was joined to an iron ring hammered into the rocks.

"Told you so. We had to know what was in there before we got too close."

The creature was twice the size of a lion, and that was what it looked like, in part. A giant crimson eagle's head grew out of the enormous shoulders of a lion's body. The long, scaly tail lashed against the cliff, sending small showers of stones down on Esti's and the children's heads. Neatly folded up along the length of its huge back were scarlet-feathered wings. The great curved beak opened, and its eerie bird calls mingled with low roarings.

"I would say it was a griffin," said Tom, "the Dragon of Wales."

"And I would say we're in trouble," continued Rory. "Look, is this really happening or what?"

"How would I know?" said Tom.

The dragon lunged forward dragging, against the chain. It guarded the only path up the sheer cliff.

"Maybe we should go around," suggested Tom.

"No. That you may not do," proclaimed the griffin in a rasping voice. "This is the only way."

"It can talk!" They were thrilled and stood gazing up at the beast in admiration.

"Of course I can talk. Do you think I am a dolt?" the griffin shrieked. "Come along, step this way!"

"I don't trust it!" said Tom, "and I am not walking anywhere near it."

"I know! Give it some meat," suggested Mackenzie. "While it's busy eating, we sneak by."

"We don't have any meat, if you haven't noticed, and you are *not* using me!" answered Rory. "I think we should throw some rocks at it and knock it out!"

"No, don't be so cruel. Couldn't we try communicating with it? Try and make friends?"

"Yes!" said Esti. "You could try. Often I have heard tales of the power of maidens over the dragon kin. But pray, do not approach too closely, Mistress."

"That's right," said Tom "It's well-known folklore. Dragons really love maidens."

"Love to eat them, I think," muttered Mackenzie.

More grunting and bellowing from above.

"Alright," she said, "but I feel like such an idiot. At least it's chained up. It won't be able to get at me."

She walked up as close as necessary without putting herself within striking distance of that beak or those claws.

"Hi!" she shouted.

The dragon became rock still. It turned its bird head to one side and stared at her unnervingly.

"Hi! Do you think we could pass by?"

A thin, silvery membrane flicked down over one eye, then retracted. The griffin swiveled its head and stared at her with the other eye, then back to the first again.

"Hi?" it repeated in disbelief. "*Hi*? What kind of greeting is that for a royal beast and a national symbol? Where is my title of respect?" It snorted and closed its eyes.

Mackenzie curtsied. "I ask pardon, your royalness."

"Granted." The griffin opened an eye.

"Permission to speak, your haughtiness?"

"I allow it." Its beak opened, and a tongue unrolled. Mackenzie wondered if it was grinning at her.

"May we have leave to walk on your pathway?"

The Griffin laughed. "Yes, you may. If you can solve a riddle."

"We'll try. Let's hear it."

No answer came back. The griffin had closed its eyes.

"The riddle?" she tried again.

"It's no use," said the griffin decidedly. "You'll never guess."

"At least let me try!"

"No point. Is it getting dark yet? My breath warms up by nightfall. I think by then I might have melted this horrid chain. Then I shall be free. By some enchantment, I know not how, I am always chained again at daybreak. But of course, you will no longer be here to see that. I shall have eaten you."

Mackenzie's spine tingled. She was beginning to think that friendship was not the key to their safe passage.

"Will you just tell me the riddle?"

The griffin shook its wings and looked out across the water. It began to hum. Mackenzie could feel herself losing her temper.

"You could at least give us a chance, especially if you're supposed to be royal. Are you a creature of honour or not?"

"Calm down! Very well, I'll pose the riddle. The answer to the riddle, of course, is my wonderful name."

The griffin swung its tail lazily from side to side and seemed to twist its beak into a smirk.

"And the riddle is?" prompted Mackenzie.

"Yes, yes. You persist so. Let me remind you, it's your doomsday. No one is going to blame me for your sad demise. I tried to dissuade you. You heard me yourself. You should go home."

"The riddle?" Mackenzie was irritated beyond endurance.

In a very self-important voice, the griffin spoke.

All know me. None escape my touch.

Disown me? Few can do as much.

"Thank you, sir," said Mackenzie through gritted teeth. She left to confer with the others.

"The clue is as good as useless," moaned Rory.

"All know me. Something everybody knows. Maybe something like the sun or, or the moon and stars," suggested Tom.

The griffin crouched on the path, listening and laughing. "Nothing heavenly. Please."

"We'll never get it," cried Rory, kicking stones in frustration.

"Come on!" howled Tom, impatient. "Just guess! Anything you can think of. How many names are there in the world anyway?"

"Yes," said Mackenzie. "We have to try."

So Esti brought forth names from his own time that they had never heard of. Rory tried some from a few of his comic books, while Mackenzie thought of some of her friends in her class. Tom reeled off names from mythologies.

"Badbh, Phantom, Geoff, Apollo . . ."

"No, no, no, no. Very cold," came the happy voice from above.

"Cedifor, Riddler, Richard, Zeus . . ."

"No, no, no, no. Freezing cold. Why, I do believe the sun is setting!"

"Feidhelm, Spiderman, Trevor, Odysseus . . ."

"No, no, no, no. Icy, icy cold."

"This is pointless," said Rory. "What I need is a weapon to defend us with. We're wasting our time thinking up stupid names."

"Be quiet!" shouted Tom. "I'm thinking. It's something we all know, right?"

"Right," said Mackenzie.

"All know me. So it's something everybody does, or has, or feels. Few escape my touch. What comes to everybody?"

"Death," suggested Mackenzie.

"No," said the griffin. "I like it, but it's not my name."

The sun was dipping below the horizon. The dragon breathed out gently, so a lick of orange flame ran along the ground. The chain glowed red in the dusk. Flames caught some of the dried-out bushes, and they flared up. In their light the dragon revealed himself, rising on his back legs and pawing the air. His claws looked like bronze in the firelight. Mackenzie felt prickles down her back as the griffin screeched in triumph.

"Don't you know what I am? If you do not guess soon, I will be having you for supper. Yum, yum!" The griffin licked its beak in anticipation.

"You are Pitiless, Merciless. You are Nightmare," cried Tom.

"Mmmmmm, getting warmer," remarked the dragon, letting out a deep sigh that devoured a small plant, "but not really."

"Heat applied to metal melts it quite fast. A chain is as strong as its weakest link." The griffin breathed on the chain again. There were a series of cracks.

"I am so scared," shivered Mackenzie. "Fear so strong I can taste it."

The dragon turned to stare at her with one eye.

"What did you say?" There was a tinge of anxiety in his voice.

In one flash it came to her. "You are Fear!" she said triumphantly. "That's your name: Fear."

"Oh, oh. No, it's not." There was a long pause. "Oh, alright, that's it. But I forgot to tell you. It doesn't count if you say it in English. You have to say it in Greek."

"That's not fair! You can't just change the rules at the end."

"Tom, what's fear in Greek?" asked Rory urgently.

"Phobos!" yelled Tom. "Your name is Phobos."

The dragon spread its wings and snorted. "All right," it said tetchily.

"Come up then. You guessed it, though I'm amazed. You may pass."

"Dare we trust it?" whispered Tom.

"There is no way back," said Esti.

They all looked back the way they had come. The water was grey and still in the twilight. The shore they had left was a faint smudge on the distant horizon.

"Come on up," croaked the griffin. "Come on, I won't eat you." Then it laughed.

CHAPTER FOUR

THE FALSE KNIGHT
ON THE ROAD

Their legs were weak and trembling, and their hearts drummed
against their sides as they climbed closer and closer.

"I don't trust it at all," muttered Rory. None of them did.

From somewhere deep inside themselves they found the strength
to keep on walking. Rory led the way, followed by Esti, who concerned himself with Mackenzie's safety. She in turn was worried
about Tom and held his hand tight as they walked.

The roarings and screechings of laughter grew louder as the
griffin watched them climb. The cruel beak opened and the long
red tongue uncurled and hung out in anticipation. They were so
close they could smell the stench of its infected breath. Suddenly, its
wings creaked open, sounding like the timbers of an old sailing ship.
As it soared into the air, its chain snapped and the griffin, now free,
hovered above them.

"You promised!" shouted Mackenzie. "We gave you your name!"

"But not in Latin or Arabic," the beast replied with a howl.

Its wings beat the air, causing a wind that sand blew into their
faces and stung their eyes. Smoke from the fires that the beast had set
off along the cliff choked them. The dragon breathed out, and flames
shot along the path in front of them, just missing Rory.

"Run! Run! Run!" screamed Esti.

They bolted along the path. They ran past the cave mouth, then followed the path as it doubled back high above the creature's lair, while the griffin swerved and soared up the cliff face after them. It sliced by Mackenzie as she ran, and its claws ripped through her jeans and tore into her skin. She felt sick with pain and fell, helpless. Paralyzed by fear, she could neither call out nor move. The beast retreated to better launch its killing attack from above. There was no hurry. He had his prey.

"Come on, Mackenzie!" Esti pulled at her. Tears washed tracks down Esti's dirty cheeks as he tried to lift her.

"I can't," she sobbed.

"If only I had something," muttered Rory.

Rory took off down the path and picked up what was left of the dragon's chain. He swung it around his head like a lasso, then let it fly. The chain arced through the air but missed the dragon. It fell clanging against the cliff until it caught on the ledge below where Tom was quivering behind a boulder.

"Ha ha de ha ha!" cried the griffin. "Missed me!" It swooped down and slashed Rory's right hand. Blood welled up from the wound.

"Rory!" yelled Esti. "Just a minute!" Esti, agile as a monkey, leapt and scrambled down the rock face and reached the chain lying on the ledge below. The griffin perched on the ledge above him watched with its head turned on one side.

"This is getting so exciting," commented the griffin. "It reminds me of when I . . ."

"Catch!" shouted Esti, hurling the chain. It spun through the air and was within Rory's reach. The griffin leapt off his ledge and lunged down at Rory to keep him from it. Rory gripped the chain in his left hand and with all his might aimed at the scaly neck. The chain hit the griffin a stinging blow on the side of the neck. The beast's great bulk hurled it into the rock face. Its wings folded, it hit the ground, rolled slowly down the cliff face, and landed on its back on the beach.

"That certainly spoilt my fun," it moaned. "I wasn't going to hurt you. I was only wanted to frighten you a little. I thought you liked being frightened. I wouldn't eat you. After all, you did guess my name."

Blood seeped through Mackenzie's torn jeans.

"It doesn't hurt much, " she said. "Rory, are you okay? Come on! Let's just go."

"Yes, I'm fine. It's just a scratch. Come on."

"Yes, do go," came a pathetic voice from the bottom of the cliff. "And please, don't go in my cave, alright? It's very private."

Esti helped Mackenzie stand, and they hurried to put as much distance between them and the dragon as they could.

"Just a minute," said Rory, hanging back. "Let's just take a quick look in cave. There might be something in there worth having."

"No! Don't!" shouted Mackenzie. "Let's just get out of here!"

Ignoring her, Rory darted back, and after checking that the griffin was still on its back, went into the darkness. He looked around but was disappointed that there was nothing to see, only an earthen floor and bare walls. As he turned to leave, he felt something underfoot. It was one of the griffin's claws, razor sharp and a bit longer than his arm. The cartilage, where it had attached to the griffin before it was shed, had hardened into a kind of hilt. The claw still had the moldy remains of previous dinners dried on to it, so Rory wiped it off on his jeans.

"Perfect!" he sighed. He ran out of the cave waving it above his head. "Look what I've got! A sword!"

"I hope it was worth risking your life for," said Mackenzie, relieved that the griffin was still lying on his back, though the beast still watched their every move.

At the top of the cliff they stopped, unsure whether the griffin would be coming after them. Mackenzie's wound was still bleeding, and Tom pressed on it down to staunch the wound. He worried about how deep it might be, but he did not want to say anything. Rory realized how serious the wound was. He turned on Esti in rage.

"Look what you've done to my sister! It's all your fault, making her come on this stupid adventure! I ought to . . ." He clenched his fist.

"Stop it," cried Mackenzie. "You're not helping."

"But *I* can help," Esti said. "This is not the reality you know at home. This is a different time and place."

"Will you shut up? Saying that over and over! I just don't get it. One minute we're in a tree, and the next minute we're here. Where are we anyway?"

"Another dimension?" suggested Tom.

Esti looked puzzled. He knelt down beside Mackenzie and looked into her eyes. "Mackenzie, if you think the wound away, it will go." She opened her mouth to protest, but her leg hurt too much.

"Close your eyes," suggested Esti. "Imagine the wound has gone. This is a dream, and you may command. Imagine the wound is healed. Repair the rip in skin and cloth."

Mackenzie closed her eyes and thought about her leg before it was sliced by the griffin.

"Look at that," cried Tom in awe as he watched the blood congeal, a scab form, and then transform into new skin. Mackenzie opened her eyes.

"It's itchy! And now it's stopped hurting!" Looking down at her leg, she cried, "Did I do that? How did that happen?"

"Try to repair thy breeches," suggested Esti.

Mackenzie closed her eyes and imagined the jeans the day she bought them. She opened her eyes and saw the ripped threads of her jeans knitting together so they looked like new.

"That is totally amazing!" Tom said in disbelief.

Rory did not say anything.

"I once dreamed that we were going to have ice cream cake for supper and guess what? We did!" said Tom finally.

"Remember that horrible dream I had?" said Mackenzie. "There was this ship sinking, and I was in the ocean trying to get into the lifeboat. I had hold of Mom, and I was trying to help her, but she couldn't breathe!" Mackenzie felt tears running down her cheeks.

"I remember you told us," said Tom, "but I forget how it ended."

"There wasn't an ending. I woke up. I think because I heard Dad calling 911 for an ambulance. What if in my dream I could have saved her! Could I change what happened to her if I changed the dream!"

Esti looked concerned. "What happened to your mother?"

Tom answered for his sister, who was struggling to wipe her tears. "Mom is in hospital. She is sleeping and can't wake up. It's called a coma when someone is like that. That's why we came to Wales for the summer. There is no one to take care of us at home. Dad is at the hospital every day."

"I pray you will suffer no more. We shall ask Merlin if he can help your mother. We can ask him when we wake him. For wake him we must. He will come to your aid, I am sure."

The three children looked at each other. Rory shook his head and mouthed, "He is *so dumb*!" But Tom and Mackenzie felt a little spark of hope in their hearts. They wanted to believe that maybe Merlin could and would help their mother.

Tenderly, Esti said, "Let us now make haste and put many furlongs between us and this place, for I fear that we may be discovered if we tarry."

"That's great," said Rory. "Another dragon, or worse?" No one replied.

They jogged down the white road that curved along the headland until the griffin was far behind them. They ran throughout the night, and as dawn came, they saw that the white road seemed to go on forever. There was no sign of life. The monotony was endless. Tom began to wonder if Esti even knew where they were going. Rory was bored stiff. And Mackenzie thought about her mother.

***

Meanwhile, Vivienne returned to the cottage at Witch's Cauldron in despair. She ran from room to room, screaming for Esti. She rifled frantically through closets stacked with the refuse of centuries. Broken armour, horses' tails dyed red, dented pewter plates and hart's horn crashed to ground.

"Come out!" she screamed. "I know you're hiding, you wretch."

She flung open chests of faded tapestries and hunted under heaps of mildewed cloaks and caps, but he was nowhere to be found. She had to admit it: Esti was gone. He had never left, not for centuries. It could only mean one thing. She fell to her knees and made a strange wolfish noise as she sobbed with rage.

"My power will dim if I lose him. I must find Esti."

She mounted her horse and galloped through the woods, along the hillside path towards the deserted quarry. There she hunted among the boulders and heaps of loose stones, listening all the while. Before long, she heard a low humming that sounded like an angry bee. She followed the sound that led her to a patch of black soil. She knew this was the place and began to dig with her nails. Sharp against her fingers, she felt a flint arrowhead as long as her palm. It was an elf bolt. She took it up with a cry of triumph, whirled around and around, and sang out these words while imagining Esti's face before her:

Elf bolt, Elf bolt, forged in forgotten mine,
Fly forward, strike him, remind him he's mine.
Sleep, hold him still, against his will.
Lead me to him, for he is mine.

She hurled the bolt with all her strength. It shrieked as it flew through a hole in the clouds, across time and space toward its target.

She listened to the sound of the elf bolt's humming across the dimensions and knew in but a little time the bolt would hit her prey, Esti.

She rode her horse straight to the stone circle on Bran's hill. From that place of power she knew the way to pass through the door between worlds. She would follow the track of the elf bolt to Esti.

***

"I am so fed up with this walking, walking and getting nowhere," announced Rory.

Tom interrupted Rory's tirade. He had noticed a ship out on the sea.

"Look at that! It's a Viking longboat!" he cried excitedly. "I always wanted to see one! There's a dragon carved as the prow."

"Silence!" Esti yelled, pulling him down on the grass. Mackenzie and Rory followed suit. They watched as the breeze freshened, the sail filled, and the boat sailed out of sight.

"They were not interested in us." Esti sighed with relief. "All the same, the road is watched. Vivienne seeks me out and has spies everywhere. Here is our plan. If we meet anyone, we will say we are on our way to render service at the blessed abbey. They will then give us safe passage. Do not stop and speak with anyone, and do not accept their gifts. They could be on her side, and they will do anything to stop us."

Rory turned to Esti and glared at him. "So now we have to have an excuse ready if someone stops and questions us. What is going to happen next? Maybe someone will try to cook us for dinner or turn us into snails the way this adventure's going. What if it turns out we can never get home!"

"I'm nervous," admitted Tom. "But it's probably okay now Rory's got a sword."

Tom looked admiringly at the sword tucked in Rory's belt.

"That was so awesome, the way you hit that griffin. Do you think I could hold your sword?"

"No, you can't," replied his brother. "Anyway, I had to do something. All *you* did was blubber."

Tom set his jaw, his face turning red. "You never give me credit for anything! You make me so mad!"

"Well, you make me just as mad! And so do you!" He glared at Esti.

"I wonder what Mom will say when you show her your sword," said Mackenzie trying to calm her brother down.

"Our mother is a vet," Mackenzie told Esti. "She looks after animals and knows all about them. Imagine the look on her face when you tell her what animal that came from!"

"I think we should go back to Aunty Maer's now," said Rory.

"But what about Merlin? I thought he was going to help us!"

"Give me a break! You believe that? This so-called game isn't much fun anymore, and on top of that, it's dangerous. Anyway, what if Dad phones us and we aren't there for the call! We've been gone for ages."

"Yes, I think we should go home too," added Tom.

Mackenzie looked at Esti's crestfallen face. "We promised we'd go with him. We can't back out now."

Esti was very quiet up to now. He took a deep breath. "Maybe I led you into danger for nothing. Perhaps you were right all along. You are not The Three. You are just three bickering children. Let us go back if that is your desire. I have no wish to bring you harm."

"Well, I'm all for that! I told you, I never even wanted to come in the first place," announced Tom.

"Should we go back?" whispered Mackenzie. "Are you sure?"

"Just spin the stone again," ordered Rory. "Let's go home."

They gathered in a circle as Mackenzie held out the stone on the chain. At the very moment she was about to spin it, Esti felt a sharp sting on his cheek that made him cry out. He fell forward like a felled tree and lay motionless on the grass. The elf bolt had struck, and Esti was in a deep, trance-like sleep.

"What's wrong, Esti?" Mackenzie, in a fright, knelt beside him.

"He's dead," announced Rory.

"Don't be an idiot," cried Tom. "He can't die! He's not even mortal!"

Suddenly, Esti turned over and tucked his knees into his chest. He let out a loud snore.

Mackenzie laughed.

"He's only asleep," she said, relieved. Then feeling angry. "Yes, but why here and now, just when we were going back? I don't like it."

Rory shouted Esti's name right in his ear while Mackenzie shook him.

"Something is very wrong," said Mackenzie with a catch in her throat. "And look, there's a mark on his cheek."

"Probably happened when he fell," guessed Tom.

"Now what are we supposed to do?" muttered Rory. "This was probably a plot all along."

"Maybe he's just tired. He's not human, after all. Maybe he always goes to sleep like this. Whatever! We can't leave him here. Let's sit and wait for him to wake up. What else can we do?"

So they sat beside him trying from time to time to wake him, but he never stirred. A long time passed, and they began to worry what they would do if Esti didn't wake up.

"We can't leave him here," said Mackenzie.

"Could we even find our way back without him?" added Tom.

The light was changing when they heard the soft beat of horse's hooves and the jingle of a bridle. Through the gloom came a heavy-set rider, clad in coal-black armour, mounted upon a black horse.

"Here's help!" cried Tom.

"Remember what Esti said. Don't tell him anything," ordered Mackenzie.

"We need help. Don't be an idiot," replied Rory who stood up to greet the stranger.

Mackenzie looked around for a place they could hide. There was nowhere to run. The rider reined in, reached behind his saddle and took out a fighting net. They watched in amazement as the man, with aim that was straight and true, threw the net and completely enveloped the children and Esti in its strands.

"Ah ha! What little fishes have we caught here?" bawled the man, laughing raucously.

They struggled and clawed, but they were trapped. The more they struggled, the louder the knight-at-arms laughed. Controlling himself with difficulty, he shouted, "What is your business on the Great White Road?"

After a pause, Tom peered through the holes in the net and spoke Esti's words, as humbly as he could. "Please, sir, we are poor travellers on our way to render service at the blessed abbey."

"That is a heap of rotting hay, whoever you are," the knight said, as he stalked over to peer through the netting. "In God's truth, this is a strange apparition!" he said when he saw Esti. "And a maiden fair, with long glistening hair." He drew himself up, tall and straight, "Now listen well! I am Madoc, the Watcher on the King's High Road, Protector of the Realm, and the Raven of Battle. Beware! In the name of the King, I charge you—and no lies now—tell me whence you come and whither you go." They were silent.

Sir Madoc stared at them. "So you need to be persuaded?" His voice was dark with menace. The knight reached inside the net and dragged out the first body he touched. It happened to be Tom. He held the boy up by the back of his sweater so he hung like a doll. Tom's eyes were level with the mad blue ones glinting beneath the cold metal helm. The knight's white animal teeth gleamed in contrast to the black curling beard. Suddenly a faraway look came into his eyes.

"I remember," he thought to himself. "I'm supposed to be courteous to the travellers on the road so they are misled and tell me all." The fierce grimace was gone, replaced by an inane grin.

"My apologies at this unseemly treatment," he said, putting Tom down. "One cannot be too wary in these uncertain times. Many are the travellers on the road who can give no good account of themselves. Jesters without a joke, minstrels without a song, peddlers without a ware." He dragged the net off his captives and invited them to sit with him. He clanked as he worked and spread his soft fleecy cloak on the ground. "Come, come, take some refreshment with me!"

They were not taken in by this sudden blossoming of courtesy. Mackenzie thought, "If we did try to make a break for it, he'd catch at least one of us." She noticed the broad cruel sword hanging at the knight's side.

"And no running away like felons, " the knight said playfully, wagging his finger at them, but there was no humour in his steely eyes. "We will sit and spin some tales together." He chuckled and looked at them craftily. "In truth, young squire, my heart warms to you." He slapped Rory on the back. "Here! Drink this for friendship's sake." He took off the drinking horn that was slung around his shoulder on a leather strap and handed it to Rory.

"Er . . . No thanks," said Rory politely.

"Go on," said the knight. "It'll make you feel better. You're probably suffering from a malaise. Just a sip and you'll feel better."

"No, that's OK," repeated Rory. "I'm feeling just fine."

"What about your companion there?" He nodded towards Esti, who was still sleeping. "Better wake him up."

"We're just letting him sleep a while," explained Mackenzie.

"Here, drink. You will feel most wonderful. This solves all problems, salves all hurts. Why, just look at me! Ever see such a fine figure of a knight? I'll wager you never have!" The knight took a swig from the horn, sighed, and laughed. "Feels better! I always think more clearly after a sip or two or three. Come on, have some. Not afraid, are you?" He pressed the horn closer to them.

Mackenzie said, "Rory, remember. You promised. You shouldn't."

Tom leaned in close to his sister's ear. "We're in a big mess now. If we act like his friends, maybe he'll help us somehow."

"You'd trust him?" she asked.

"Go on Rory," said Tom. "I'll have some if you do. Don't know what else we're supposed to do."

Rory caved in. He held up the horn and squirted the tiniest drop he could into his upturned mouth. At once, he felt as if his throat had been bitten by a snake. As Rory spluttered, the knight roared with delight. "Ah yes! The sweetness of honey but the breath of a dragon. Such is a brew from the King's high hall. Have some more!"

Rory felt warmth trickling through his body. He smiled at the knight who now looked such a sweet and gentle person. "He's alright, really," he said.

Mackenzie glared at Rory. "How can you be so stupid? Why are you acting so dumb!" Meanwhile, the knight took no notice of her, bending all of his attention toward the two boys.

"Yes, I've had enough of doing what Esti wants. Esti this and Esti that. We are going back home, but that will be later on. Right now I would really like a little more of that mead, if I may, Sir," said Rory politely.

Madoc handed him the horn and made a big grin. Rory had no hesitation this time and drank deeply. He was disappointed when Madoc retrieved the drinking horn and handed it to Tom.

"See how those that do not drink do not share our pleasure?" remarked Madoc, nodding at Tom.

Tom gingerly took a sip, as it seemed to be such a big hit. He could hardly believe how sweet it was! It glided down his throat like liquid sunlight. At the same time his head cleared. It was as though his mind had snapped awake. Rows and rows of equations started to dance through his mind.

"Mackenzie! I've just figured out the solution to x+y=n! The answer is purple curtains. I have been on the wrong track! "

Mackenzie sighed and shook her head. Tom took another sip.

"Hey! I've finally figured out how to make a pair of binoculars out of cucumbers!"

"Stop it, Tom! Just stop it!"

Madoc leaned over and patted Tom's shoulder. "Take no notice of the wench. The wonders of this brew never cease to amaze those who drink deeply. Ideas become brilliant."

"I really don't think so," interrupted Mackenzie.

"And as for you Rory, how warmly you embrace my friendship. Now share all with me."

"Oh, I definitely do!" agreed Rory.

"You know what, my boy? Because now we are so close in kinship and because you like my horn of mead, I will tell a secret. That old horn belonged to Merlin."

"Then how come you've got it, if it's supposed to be Merlin's?" asked Mackenzie.

"Well, the old fool doesn't need it anymore, considering where he finds himself right now." Madoc allowed himself a snigger. Rory joined in, giggling and threw his arms around the knight's neck.

"Now tell me, brave squire," Madoc questioned. "What brings you to the road? Some special venture, I would hazard."

"*That* I cannot divulge. Not even to you."

"Come now, squire. You can tell an old friend. Why do you hesitate? Perhaps you do not trust me?" He sighed woefully.

"It's just that I made a promise to *him*." Rory nodded towards Esti.

Madoc started to laugh and jeer. "To him! A great warrior like you, swearing fealty to a funny looking creature who couldn't swing a sword? You must have your reason if you bend a knee to one such as that. Not scared of him, are you? Does he have you under a spell?"

"No, you've got it all wrong, Madoc. I don't take orders from him!"

"Then tell me your adventure, squire. After all, maybe I can help you."

"Rory, stop it!" screamed Mackenzie. "You'll put us all in danger."

Rory stood up. "Oh, and I suppose Esti hasn't? Dragging us off who knows where? We're attacked by a dragon-thing and then he falls asleep on us. And that's *after* he begs us to free Merlin and save the world! He's been messing with us this whole time."

"Sit down, Squire," soothed Madoc. "Merlin you say?" His voice was almost squeaky with excitement. "Tell me all about it."

Mackenzie felt powerless against the wiles of the metal-encased man. Her eyes lingered with horror on his prickly, blood-flecked spurs. Tom shared her horror. He had only had a sip of the mead, and luckily for him, his head had already cleared. His great ideas of a moment ago were now embarrassing. But Rory was fully under the power of the knight.

So Rory recklessly told Madoc all he knew about the quest. But when he mentioned that they were running away from the evil enchantress, Vivienne, the knight thundered and his face blackened. His startled horse whinnied and put its ears back as he bellowed, "You have been sorely misled! Indeed, you do her wrong. I well know this lady of whom you speak, and she deserves this not. It is some trumped-up charge." His hand was on the pommel of his sword. He unsheathed it and slashed at a nearby shrub. There was a hushed silence as they all tensed.

In the commotion, Tom reached over and took the horn of mead and shoved it down the front of his jacket without Madoc noticing. "I'm going to make sure he doesn't use this brew on anyone else. And certainly he is not giving Rory any more," he thought to himself.

"Well, of course, I'm only going by what Esti says," Rory shouted nervously to Madoc.

"Oh *him*," sneered Madoc. "What does that creature know about it anyway? He is beneath my notice, an unworthy opponent." Madoc finally pulled himself together.

"I shall attend only to you, squire, for I wish to learn more of your adventure. Now, you say that you want to wake that old druid, Merlin. It is your great good fortune that our paths crossed. You see, Merlin is an old fool, and it is best he should be incarcerated in a large rock. His time was over and done long ago. Let's get on with progress, the future. Leave things alone that you do not understand."

"You're right," said Rory with conviction. "I'm taking everyone back to Penrith Wood."

Madoc laughed. "Penrith Wood, you say? If you are on your way there, you have no time to waste. Listen. I know the way. It is so quick and easy! You see the stream over there?" He pointed to a thin silver thread in the distance. "Cross it, and follow it inland and northward. It flows through Penrith Wood. You'll be home soon enough."

Tom perked up. Finally they were going home.

Rory leapt to his feet, ready to leave. Mackenzie grabbed hold of his arm, "Wait! How do you know he is telling us the truth!"

"Shut up," shouted Rory, the mead having removed his last shred of good sense. "I'm leading now, so come on! Inland and north it is!"

"Rory, wait!" cried Mackenzie. "You can't leave Esti!" She grabbed hold of Esti and shook him vigorously. "Wake up Esti!" How on earth could they wake him?

"Who cares about Esti," shouted Rory. "We're going without him. We know the way back now, and we don't need him." Rory was already some distance away from the little group.

"Rory, don't go!" cried Tom.

"Esti!" screamed Mackenzie. "Get up! Tom, please do something!"

"Mackenzie, Tom, just come! Leave him there!"

"There is one thing you could do," said Tom. "It's the only thing I can think of. From an old fairy story."

Mackenzie caught his hesitation, "Just say it! What?"

"Kiss him!"

"Kiss him? *Kiss him!* Okay." Mackenzie kissed Esti on the cheek, right on the red mark they had noticed. "Maybe I can kiss it better," she thought.

At that moment, Esti's green eyes sprang open. "What's happening?"

He sat up and saw Rory in the distance, heading northwards. "No! No! What is he doing!" He leapt up and raced after Rory. Tom ran too and Mackenzie after him.

"Oh look, the funny little fellow woke up! That's the spirit," the knight shouted after them, pulling his visor down to hide his evil grin. "Make haste! Forward and farewell."

"Tis fortunate for My Lady, for they shall never find the old fool Merlin in the place where they are going, nor will they find the road home," he mused. "Now where did I put my mead? I was going to celebrate a little."

Esti, Tom, and Makenzie caught up with Rory, who finally slowed down to wait for them.

"Had a nice nap?" drawled Rory.

"It's Vivienne," cried Esti. "She enchanted me!"

"It doesn't matter now. We're going home anyway." Rory again picked up the pace and stalked towards the stream.

"Stop! Let's make sure we're going the right way!" cried Tom but Rory gave him his customary reply, "Shut up Tom."

Mackenzie now moved in front of Rory. "Let's talk this through with Esti. He can help us get home."

"I've had enough of Esti and his hare-brained plans. All I can say is it's lucky for us that we met Madoc."

"Please don't go that way! Mackenzie, help me stop him!" Esti got hold of Rory, who thumped him with his shoulder. Esti fell. Mackenzie and Tom went to help him up. Rory kept going. He was already fording the stream to cross to the track that ran beside it. Once he crossed, they watched in horror. A thick cloud of swirling mist engulfed Rory, and he vanished.

"Where's he gone?"" screamed Mackenzie. "What do we do now?"
"Make haste!" cried Esti. "We needs must find him and bring him back before he goes further. Who knows what danger lies ahead."

The three of them reached the stream, thrashed through the icy cold water, and a cold, swirling mist enclosed them too. A cold blanket of darkness fell. Mackenzie grabbed Esti's hand while she still knew where he was.

"Rory! Tom!" Mackenzie called into the darkness. She and Esti reached out this way and that, but there was not even one spark of light. They could see nothing. Mackenzie panicked and soon lost all sense of direction. It was a relief when she almost tripped on a warm body.

"I'm here, Mackenzie," came a sad voice. It was Tom.

Then she heard, "Where on earth are we?" and recognized Rory's voice. "I can't find the stream anywhere."

Blind and helpless, the children and Esti were alone in the darkness. In the distance they could hear the howls and cries of strange animals. An icy wind sighed around them. They had no idea how to go back the way they came nor which direction to go forward.

"We are lost," said Esti. His voice sounded heavy with defeat. "We are lost for eternity. You have been tricked. We have left the true path and catapulted into the wrong time and place."

CHAPTER FIVE
THE BEGINNING OF TIME

"Where is he?" Vivienne appeared suddenly on the road before Madoc, who was now remounted on his black stallion. The animal reared in terror at the sudden apparition.

Madoc dismounted and grinned apishly. "My Lady Vivienne!" he cried and bowed on bended knee. Vivienne controlled her desire to kick him.

"Get up, you oaf. Where is my—my little slave boy? You know, the small, ugly one?" She glanced up at the saddlebags as if Esti were stowed away in one of them. Madoc thought for a moment.

"Oh yes! You mean the company with the strange boy." He laughed. "I sent them packing."

Vivienne struggled to master her fury. "You idiot! You dolt! You numbskull! Why did you not detain them? Why was he on the road? Where is he now? Tell me!" she screamed.

Madoc pouted, folded his arms, and turned his back on her. "You are ill-natured, My Lady, to speak so sorely to one who seeks only your favour. I will tell you no more."

Vivienne quickly changed her tactics. "Sire," she said sweetly as a trickle of honey, "you are so bold and gallant. Pray, forgive my anger. The loss of the one I seek distresses me more that you can know."

Madoc, somewhat mollified, turned back. Vivienne, pursuing her advantage, took a glove of white calfskin from her hand and gave it to the knight.

"Take my favour, brave knight. Serve only me, and I shall be your lady."

Madoc blushed with pleasure and bowed low again. Vivienne tapped her foot.

"He was with two young squires and a damsel of no account."

The blood drained from Vivienne's face. "And where were they going?"

Madoc explained. "They said they would wake the wizard Merlin, imprisoned in the rock by your skill, My Lady."

"No!" she screamed. "I have to get to the wood of Broceliand before them. I must ride!" She pulled herself onto the saddle behind Madoc. The horse whinnied and reared in terror.

"Not so swift, My Lady. Listen well. I have done my duty. The company will never reach where Merlin is imprisoned. For their insult to you, I sent them north. They will soon be hopelessly lost on the icefields. It will be long ere they return to hearth and kin, if they ever do."

"They can wander forever for all I care, but I must find Esti and take him home with me. You may accompany me."

"My Lady, I will do your bidding. I will go with you to the end of time—to the end of the world! I would gladly lay down my life for you."

A speculative look came into her eyes. "Well, if you insist," she said and laughed.

***

Mackenzie held on to Rory, who held Esti, who held Tom. It was the only way they could reassure themselves that they were not alone. Suddenly they saw something shimmer in the sky, colours like a long trailing scarf of light. They could make out each other's faces reflecting the coloured lights. It was a relief.

"Aurora Borealis," said Tom. "We must be quite far north."

"This doesn't look like the way home," said Rory.

"You mean you thought that knight was trying to help us?" Mackenzie asked in disbelief, her voice growing louder. "You actually thought this was the way home?"

Rory groaned. "Don't shout. My head hurts. I don't remember."

"Oh yes, you do," answered Tom.

"How are we ever to find our way out of this? What are we supposed to do?" Tom looked to Rory for an answer.

"At least I didn't go to sleep, like some people," answered Rory. "At least I was trying to help us get somewhere."

Mackenzie stuck up for Esti. "It wasn't his fault Vivienne put a spell on him."

"Come on," said Esti, noticing the sky was slowly lightening in the east as the sun rose. "It is dawn. Let us journey on and face what fate might send us."

They set off into the dead world. There was no song of bird, no murmur of water, no whisper of wind, only the ominous silence of a sterile stillness. Moisture frozen in the air shone like silver darts.

"It must be bitterly cold, but I don't feel cold," murmured Mackenzie.

"It's like a dream," said Esti. "We're here in thought but not in body. It can only hurt you if you believe it can. Cold is a dangerous enemy. It will try to creep in if you let it. It wants to invade your mind and pinch you with its icy fingers."

Mackenzie's eyes felt red and hot from the constant white glare. Soon all of them were hypnotized by the blank stillness.

Tom thought to himself, "I wonder how cold it is. If we could feel it, we could guess. Water freezes at 0 degrees Celsius, so it must be below that. Mercury freezes at -40 in Fahrenheit or Celsius. What would it be like to feel that cold? I suppose my feet and hands would go numb first." He suddenly stopped thinking and said, "My hands and feet are a bit cold."

Esti looked worried. "Look at his face!" The skin on Tom's nose and cheeks was bloodless white. He was freezing.

"You were thinking about the cold. You were making it real!"

"Tom, stop thinking about it!" Mackenzie shook him.

"Now I started, I don't know how to stop!"

Mackenzie and Rory took off their jackets to wrap around their brother.

"It will not help," said Esti. "The cold is in his mind. Nothing will make him feel any warmer but escape from this place."

High above, two ravens screamed as they spiraled down to land on a ridge of ice beside Esti and the children. They were the size of two small dogs. Both birds turned their heads sideways to stare at the four.

"Friend or foe?" muttered Rory. "Probably something else out to get us."

"Maybe they're just birds," suggested Mackenzie.

"Nothing is ever what it seems. Not around here anyway," Rory warned.

They looked across a panorama of white hills that crawled into the distance like the humped backs of white whales, without beginning and without end. A huge fragment of ice, the size of a cathedral, broke away from the hill and smashed down into the ice valley. It shattered like a piece of glass. The earth shuddered, and they heard a loud groan. It came from a heap of black rags in front of them. The ravens cawed in terror, flew upwards, and disappeared.

Slowly the pile of rags unraveled, revealing a woman with a face so old and wrinkled that if someone had said she was a thousand years old, they would have believed it. Her hands were white and thin as parchment, knotted with thick ropes of blue veins. Her iron-grey hair was braided. The black rags were her dresses and petticoats and cloaks, of which she wore layers uncounted. They started in amazement when she greeted them,

"All hail, Travellers," she croaked. Her voice was loud and echoed on the ice around. As she spoke, they all felt the cold seep into their minds.

"All hail," said Esti respectfully. The others followed his lead.

"We are lost," said Mackenzie. "Can you help us find a way?"

"You need a direction, and all directions meet in me. I am everywhere and nowhere, and for now I am the Lady of the North." The old woman wheezed with laughter. Then she chanted like a mindless machine:

> My lungs of stone
> Send breath to kill.
> My heart of stone
> Destroys your will,
> Strikes like a knife.
> Cruel cold steals life.

She reached out her hand like a claw and held Tom by his shoulder.

"I will give you a direction, but you must pay." Tom crumpled beneath her touch.

"Hey! Hands off him!" Rory quickly stepped forward and tried to wrench the old woman's hand away, but it held as tightly as metal pincers. The old woman's breath filled the air with hoarfrost that stroked their hair. What it touched, it coated with ice. Mackenzie's long, dark hair turned white.

"I will pay whatever she asks," sobbed Rory. "Look at Tom! What is going to happen to us if we don't get out of here? I know it's my fault we're lost."

The old woman released Tom, and Rory struggled to hold him upright. Tom tried hard to keep his eyes open as the cold dragged him toward eternal sleep, but he could not.

"A sacrifice," the old woman said, now pleased, and threw down her stone knife like a challenge.

"What do you want us to do with that?" asked Mackenzie in horror.

"If you wish to leave this place where time began, then you must give me what you most prize."

"It has all gone wrong because of me!" Esti burst out. "I should have waited for the real three to come! I brought you into danger that was beyond your strength and powers." He sank down on his heels and covered his face with his sleeve. "I am sorry," he cried.

Rory took charge. "Look, what is the point of going on about that now? What have we got to give her? Look in your pockets"

"I have my necklace." Mackenzie began to undo it.

"No!" Esti looked up. "You can't. You will all need it if you are to get home again. Do not part with it."

"Well, what else have we got?" asked Rory.

"Tom has his bird spotter's book and a pencil," volunteered Mackenzie.

Tom struggled to pull it out of his pocket.

"No, Mom gave him that book before the accident. He can't part with that." Rory was adamant. Mackenzie looked at Rory in surprise.

"Well, that's new," she thought, "Rory thinking about Tom for a change."

"I have this horn of mead," whispered Tom.

The crone shook her head. "I know that horn is not yours!" she cried.

"What do we do? Esti has nothing. He doesn't even have a pocket, never mind anything to put in it."

"There's one thing." Rory took out his pride and joy, his dragon's claw sword.

He held it out to the old woman's open hand.

"No!" cried Esti. "How can you be a warrior without a sword?"

"I'd rather have my brother than a sword," Rory said, looking away. The crone ignored him. Her eyes were on Mackenzie. "Your hair!" cried the crone. "Your hair." And as she stretched out her hand, Mackenzie saw a sickle clutched in her fingers, glinting like a silver moon.

"My hair?" whispered Mackenzie. "You want to cut off my hair?" The crone laughed. It was decided.

Mackenzie closed her eyes and felt the tugging of the little sickle as it cut through every strand. Soon her beautiful hair lay black on the ice.

The old woman took the hair and threaded it back and forth across the sickle that was no longer sharp but white and smooth as bone. Back and forth she worked until she had made a harp. She ran her fingers over the strings made of Mackenzie's hair, and the sound was eerie, sweet, and full of longing.

Then the crone laughed and raised her arms heavenward. She cried out "Adumlah! Adumlah!" They heard a sound they never thought to hear in that ice-bound land: the lowing of a cow. Over an icy brow appeared a fat red-and-white cow. As she began to lick the ice with obvious enjoyment, the woman sang softly, plucking the strings of the hair to accompany her.

Salt's sting,
Salt's bite.
Sting will heal.
Bite is clean.
Pure Salt
Salt white.
Too much is death.
Enough is life.
Salt in sea,
Salt in ice,
In eons past
Created life.

The cow's long pink tongue went in and out, and soon they were looking at a pool of water in a hollow of ice. Rory bent down and rubbed his finger along the sheet of ice and tasted it. The ice was salty. "We must be standing on a frozen sea," he said. The cow licked on, and the pool overflowed in four directions. The four tiny streams melted the ice at such a rate they were soon four fast-moving rivers eating into the ice, growing deeper and deeper. The musical sound of running water was so exciting after the frozen silence. At last the cow lifted her head and ambled out of sight.

"Choose," said the Crone. "Choose one river, for each is a direction."

"The River of the West," answered Esti.

Then the old woman took off one black cloak. She unwound it, and it grew like a black bandage until it lay across the ice. Then she lifted it, faced the River of the North, and flapped the cloak up and down. A breeze ruffled their hair a little, but as the old lady lifted it again, the cloak billowed out like a sail, and the breeze blew harder and whistled as it came. This was her song to the north wind:

Storm Bringer, Cloud Chaser,
Send forth thy Power.
Your breath will chill,
It lies so still.
Ice is thy Dower.

The wind growled and raged and moaned and screamed. The children had to cling hard to each other just to stand upright. Then the River of the North was no more. It returned to ice and was one with the glacier again.

The Lady of the North turned to the River of the East. As she did, she became a thin, black shadow. In her place stood a young, dark girl. She was very beautiful but stern and dressed in flowing silks of crimson and blue. In her ears were great hoops of gold, and her arms were heavy with jewel-encrusted bracelets. Her bare feet rested on orange sand. The children felt a blast of hot air hit them in the face. Off in the distance they thought they could see palm trees and yellow silk tents. They heard the hypnotic sound of a flute, accompanied by little chiming bells. The woman held the cloak and sang to the east wind in a husky voice as the cloak lifted and fell.

Heat Hazer, Dust Raiser,
Send forth thy Power.
Your Breath is steam,
No longer seen.
Mists are thy dower.

The children felt hotter and hotter. Their throats were dry, and their clothes stuck to them. Huge dust clouds rose up like pillars, and sand blew everywhere. The intense heat evaporated the water of the River of the East, and soon it was no more. Sand quickly filled in the channel where the river had once been. The desert was dry.

The Lady of the East turned and faced the River of the South. A subtle change took place, and they saw only her back. As the Lady of the South, she wore a flowing yellow robe spangled with flowers. Her hair was bright gold and hung down to her waist. The sights and sounds of the east were gone, and it seemed to them the lady stood in a lush green field. The trees about her were full of birds. Butterflies and bees caressed the flowers in the grass. They could hear crickets singing and frogs croaking, plopping their little green bodies into the river. A skylark soared, trilling with joy. The lady held the cloak and moved it up and down. She sang to the south wind in a sweet, lilting voice.

Bird Bringer,
Sun Singer,
Send forth thy Power.
Let Earth drink deep.
In soil will seep.
Marsh is thy Dower.

The children could smell the scents of summer: flowers in full bloom, mown hay, ripening fruit. The soft breeze barely ruffled the surface of the river, but it was fast sinking, as if someone had pulled the plug. Soon there was nothing left except a muddy ditch in the meadow. Small green shoots poked their way up through the soil towards the light.

The whole scene disappeared as if someone had turned off a light. The Lady of the East turned to face the River of the West. She became as a silhouette, reappeared, and changed again. Now she was the Lady of the West and wore soft folds of purple velvet. Her hair of red-gold ringlets was entwined with leaves of flaming red, bright copper, and amber. About her feet were sheaves of wheat, plump pumpkins, small russet apples, and dusky grapes. In the distance were orchards groaning with the weight of fruit and fields of heavy-headed grain. The meandering River of the West was sheltered by thick woods, their leaves a riot of fall colours. They seemed to have set the sky on fire, for the clouds smoldered vermilion, crimson, and rose. A flock of silver-winged geese flew high overhead, and their melancholy cry signaled their leave-taking.

The lady turned towards Esti and the children and beckoned to them to enter her world. They felt drawn to her, and as they came close, she greeted them. "All hail, travellers!"

Rory helped Tom to his feet and held him tight. The Lady took the horn that once was Merlin's and breathed upon it. Then she held it to Tom's white lips. He smelled the warm, golden scents of fruits which wafted around her.

"Drink this," she said softly. "This is no longer the brew of madness but of solace and strength."

"This time, Tom, I know it's safe to drink. I swear I will never lead you into danger again," murmured Rory.

Tom drank deeply. The water of the west surged through his body, warming him. His mind healed. When he looked into the face of the lady, he thought for one moment that he looked into his mother's eyes. Just as quickly, the fancy was gone.

"Take this horn now filled with the liquid of wisdom and enlightenment. The horn may be Merlin's, but the drink is thine own," the lady promised.

Tom slung the strap that held the horn across his chest. Then the Lady of the West turned to Mackenzie and handed her the harp made from the sickle and from her long black hair. "This belongs to the Singer," she said. "The time comes when you shall need it."

Mackenzie found the bone harp so light she hardly felt its weight as it hung on her shoulder.

The lady turned to Rory and said, "This day you began to be the Warrior who protects those he loves." The lady touched the sword hanging from his belt. Straight away there came a flash of light, and the sword was encased in a golden sheath. "Farewell, Thought Travellers," she said.

They followed her gaze down to the river where a small rowboat bobbed up and down on the water.

"The boat will take you to the wood of Broceliand. Or else it will take you home. Your choice. And so I take my leave. You have met one few have seen." She smiled, and for a moment they saw the old woman they had first met. Then she was gone, and she was the Lady of the West again. She laughed as she sang,

> *Four in One.*
> *One in Four.*
> *One is all.*
> *All is one.*

Esti and the three children scrabbled down the slippery bank and climbed aboard the boat. Two ravens flew high above, as though watching them. "I wonder if they are the same two ravens we saw before," Mackenzie thought to herself. "No, they couldn't be."

"Where do you want to go?" asked Esti, certain he was speaking to the Singer, the Sage, and the Warrior. "Do you still want to go home?"

"Let's finish what we started," said Rory. Tom and Mackenzie agreed. "We are not quitters!"

The boat had a white sail, which filled with the wind blowing them toward their destiny. The swiftly moving current carried them forward at such a pace that soon the Lady of the West was just a golden speck on the distant horizon.

CHAPTER SIX
THE TIN MINE

The little boat carried them swiftly through a warm valley with thickly wooded slopes. Esti felt the warm sun on his face, and he smiled to think how far they had come. They would be in Broceliand soon. Vivienne would not suspect their plan, and surely she would never find them. Squinting up at the cloudless sky, Esti saw two ravens, riding on the air currents high above.

"Is that a bear?" cried Tom, pointing excitedly.

Esti laughed. "No, it's one of the brothers from the abbey."

Tom looked embarrassed. "It's not my fault I can't see very well," he muttered, adjusting his glasses. Rory patted Tom on the shoulder. "It's okay."

As they passed, the monk looked up from gathering blackberries and waved. It was too late to duck down in the boat, so Esti waved back. The boat moved so fast on the current that the monk was soon far behind.

The boat brought them closer to a range of hills. Esti told them the tallest one was the Beacon. Beside it was Bran's Hill with its circle of standing stones on top, like a crown. Their size and shape made each stone resemble a group of people, watching and waiting.

"There are many hidden doors between worlds, and the stone circle is one. In your world no one cares too much about stone circles anymore. Farmers used to break them up and use the stones to build walls. Even so, they still they contain magic."

"You mean like the tree hit by lightning? Doors between worlds?"

"Yes, and much more."

The boat slowed as the river widened.

"It's better to go on foot now," said Esti. "I think we are near." He grabbed some willow branches that dipped down into the water, and the boat glided into the muddy bank. They had arrived in the wood of Broceliand, just as the lady of the four directions had promised.

They climbed out of the boat and found themselves in a forest of silver birch trees. Autumn leaves shone like gold coins against the cloudless blue sky. Next they noticed the silence. Not even a bird sang. "It's as though the whole wood is asleep," whispered Mackenzie. She wore her harp on her shoulder, Rory took his sword in hand, and Tom tucked his horn under his belt. They fell in line behind Esti, who followed deer tracks that wound through a maze of rusty ferns. The tracks took them deeper and deeper into the woods.

It was late afternoon when they came upon a fountain in the middle of a little glade. Clear water shot up out of a stone lion's mouth. It sparkled in the sunlight and cast rainbows of light. The spray splashed into a large basin below the lion. Curiously, there was no sound of running water. The children and Esti saw that the water on one side of the basin was pure and clear but on the other side black and smelled of rotting weeds. The two waters remained side by side, separated by an invisible barrier.

Rory reached out his hand to put it into the water.

"Stay!" cried Esti. "Words are carved in the stone."

They could see very faint indentations on the stone lip of the basin. Mackenzie pored over them and read:

This water sweet is offered you,
Travellers who are brave and true,
To open ears and open eyes,
To know what in this clearing hides

This water foul is all that's due
To travellers who would evil do.
To shut their ears and make them blind,
Sojourning in Broceliand.

"*What's sojourning?*" *said Mackenzie, looking at Tom.*

"Travelling," was the reply. "So that's why it's so quiet! We have to drink the pure water, and then we can actually see everything that is in the wood and hear everything too!"

"Yes, if we are brave and true. That's what it says."

"Let's risk it!" Rory insisted. "Whatever faults any of us have, I don't think we count as evil."

"I'm going to drink," Mackenzie decided. "I think we need to know exactly what is hiding in the forest!"

"I'm in," said Tom, "as long as there are no bears."

"No guarantee there!"

With one mind all four cupped their hands, filled them with water, and sipped. The moment they drank they heard a loud pop in their ears like a balloon bursting. They suddenly heard a great fanfare as the wood burst into life. The birdsong was deafening.

"Listen! I can hear a fox!" cried Tom. "And insects twittering away."

The wood, which had been so still, was alive with animals. A field mouse scampered past their feet, a spider spun webbing in the grass, deer grazed in the glade, squirrels leapt from tree to tree, and a flock of geese honked overhead.

They noticed two ravens perched on a tree some distance away, and above the forest sounds they could hear what strangely seemed to be human voices. The first voice was malicious and cold, the second rough and syrupy sweet.

The first said, "Ha! I can see them. They have stopped to rest. Now we have them!"

The second replied, "Dearest Lady, you see so well with your little raven eyes. What do you want me to do now? Shall I run them through with a sharp, pointed instrument?"

"It's Vivienne!" cried Esti in terror.

"And I remember that other voice," added Mackenzie. "It's Madoc. But where on earth are they?"

They looked around them but were unable to see any sign of their enemies.

"Let's stay where we are," said Rory decisively. "At least right now we're in a position of defense. We'll be able to see where they're coming from. If we have to, we can make a dash or else stand our ground here." He held his sword in front of him, and Tom stood beside him.

The ravens flew to the next tree, a little nearer to the fountain.

"There's something very odd about those ravens," said Rory. "I don't quite know. Could be nothing. The shadows are playing tricks on my eyes."

The two ravens took a low flight across the glade but did not land. In their places were two human-shaped shadows that flitted among the tree trunks, coming around the glade to their right. One was broad and heavy and the other long and thin. Both moved with determination, then stopped. Indeed, it was Vivienne and Madoc. They could hear the knight's breath rasping in and out, like a wild animal longing to attack.

"Shall we run?" squealed Tom.

"Yes, then at least we'll have a chance." Mackenzie took Tom's hand but stopped in her tracks when a chill voice split the air.

"Esti, come here! I shall punish you for this disobedience."

"I beg you, let me be, Mistress!"

"No, Esti. You belong to me. Mine forever!"

Esti stood rock still, paralyzed by Vivienne's presence and mesmerized by her voice. The force of habit, centuries old, took hold of him, and he took a step towards her.

"Yes, Mistress, I am coming."

Mackenzie grabbed him, saying his name over and over as if to wake him from sleep. The touch of a friend made him turn to her, and for an instant, the spell was broken.

Vivienne's eyes narrowed, and she changed her tactics. She called out "Esti" in a voice as sweet as rotting fruit. "What little game are you playing? Do you really think you can escape me?"

"No, Mistress," he whispered.

Then Vivienne laughed shrilly, cutting into their senses like a razor.

"You think you will be able to free Merlin? A fool's errand. None will ever free him from the rock, least of all a useless being like yourself and your three little friends. You are all nothing!"

All the time she spoke, she inched forward, stalking her prey. She never took her eyes off Esti. Her long skirts trailed behind so that she seemed to glide, very slowly and surely. As she came nearer and nearer, Rory very carefully cupped his hand in the foul fountain water and waited. Vivienne reached out her hand, almost touching Esti. Her mouth was turned up in triumph. Madoc's shoulders shook in silent amusement as he enjoyed the scene. In his hand was a double-headed axe, and every now and then he ran his thumb along the blades.

Vivienne took one more step, and Rory splashed her. The water hit her full in the face.

"Run!" Rory yelled, and they took off into the trees. The enchantress' shrill screams of terror rang in their ears as they ran. Madoc threw his axe after them, and it sang through the air, luckily straight into a tree trunk.

Madoc went to comfort his lady, now lying on the grass, her face wet.

"I can't see, you fool! Where are you? Speak to me. I cannot hear you!"

"My Lady, I am beside you."

"Speak to me, you oaf!" she screamed. "Why can I not see? I command you, raven, chase after them!"

Madoc obeyed. He stretched out his arms, and between hand and leg grew a curtain of black feathers. His nose and chin lengthened and joined into a beak. Then he shrank smaller and smaller, growing feathers all the while. His legs became scaly and his feet turned into claws. Having shape-shifted into his raven form, he knew he would soon catch up with his prey.

"The raven flies again!" he cried aloud.

"Have you gone yet, you oaf? Hurry back with them. Then take me away from this place. I fear the magic here is stronger than I."

***

The four of them ran through the trees so fast that Mackenzie thought her lungs would burst. Hearts raced in terror.

"I have to stop," cried Tom. "I can't keep up!"

Mackenzie dragged him behind her. "We can't stop, Tom."

Tom fell over, exhausted. Through the trees behind them was a shadow flying in pursuit.

"Something's following us!" screamed Mackenzie.

Rory ran back. "Quick, there's somewhere ahead where we can hide. You can make it. It's just a little farther." Mackenzie and Rory helped Tom as best they could. There, ahead of them, was a small open shaft going down into the earth. The hole was surrounded by rotting timbers. A rope, tied to a boulder, dropped down into the dark hole. Hot musty air breathed out of it.

There was no time to hesitate. One by one they climbed down the rope. The earth was soft and made toe-holds all the way to the bottom. There they found themselves in a tunnel that seemed to go on for miles. It was lit by a ghostly green light.

Rory was the last down, and as he touched the ground, the rope snapped, snaked down, and coiled in a heap at their feet.

"It must have been rotten," said Rory. "We were lucky to get down. But on the other hand, how are we going to get out again?"

Esti picked up the end of the rope and noticed the end had been deliberately cut. He did not want to alarm them, so he said nothing. At least they would not be followed.

There were rich veins of metal running in seams along the length of the tunnel, and it was these that gave off the eerie green light. When they looked at each other, they saw their skin reflect back the greenness; they all looked like vegetables. The tunnel smelled of growing things. It was easy to imagine they could hear the roots drinking.

"It looks like an old tin mine," said Tom.

All of them, except Esti, felt light-headed after their escape.

"We're safe now!" Tom cried. "These mines always have an exit, and we can just follow the tunnel to the surface. Vivienne and her sidekick will never be able to track us down here."

"Hello! Hello!" They called and giggled. The echo came back, *"Lo! Lo!"*

"Will you keep quiet?" whispered Esti, looking back.

"Oh, Esti. Give us a break. We can't laugh? Don't be such a spoil sport," Rory answered, then shouted out, "Can you hear me?"

"Can you . . . can you . . . can you . . . HEAR ME?" The echo was very loud. It came again. *"I can hear you . . . hear you . . . hear you."*

"That was really weird," Tom commented. "Is that exactly what you shouted, Rory?"

"I don't think so."

"I'm scared!" whispered Mackenzie.

"Scared?" whispered the echo in reply.

"How soon do you think we can get out of here?"

"Out of here? Out of here?"

"It won't be long," promised Tom hopefully. He recently read a book about mines.

"Beware . . . beware . . . beware . . . beware."

Mackenzie was really spooked and looked around. It did not feel as though they were alone.

"Just be quiet," insisted Esti. "I pray, please stop talking."

"I sort of wish we hadn't come down here now," Tom muttered

"Will you stop talking!" cried Esti again.

Rory felt he had to speak up for himself. "We had no choice but hide down here. What else were we supposed to do? We had to take our chance."

"A chance . . . a chance . . . Don't dance . . . Don't dance . . ."

Rory pulled himself together. "It's nothing but our echo." He shouted in defiance, "It's just us."

There was a pause.

"It's just me, " came back the tinny voice of the echo.

"I warned you!" Esti struggled to stay calm. "There is something down here, and now it is in no doubt that there are strangers in its precincts."

They stopped talking altogether and walked quietly along the warm, dry tunnel, past the seams of metallic light. Then, very faintly, they heard a sound: *tap tap tap.* It grew louder and louder. It was not possible to tell where it was coming from. The best plan seemed to be to run, but their haste only brought them closer to the source of the sound. Around the next bend they saw a dozen little men busily chipping at the rich veins of tin. They were stripped to the waist and wore dusty brown breeches and leather aprons that hung down to their very large bare feet. Thick bands of brown cloth were tied around their heads to keep their long, curly locks out of their eyes. From each chin grew a bushy beard. The miners were so engrossed in their work they did not notice the children, so Rory signaled the others to creep on by. They pressed their backs against the tunnel wall and began to inch along. It was fairly wide at that point, and they were able to get almost past the little men when they noticed that although the miners puffed and panted and looked serious, they had very little to show for their efforts.

At that moment, the biggest miner flung down his pick and announced in a thunderously loud voice, "Well now, brothers! Time for the feast! Let down the tools!"

The whole crew dropped their tools and wiped their faces on their shirts, which they then put on.

"We worked hard today, brothers," said another. "We deserve a rest and our dinner."

"We deserve a dinner and our rest," they chorused.

From the fumblings and bumpings that followed, it was obvious that the little men were very short-sighted. It was no wonder the four of them had managed to creep past. Although the little men could not see well, they more than made up for it with a pair of very large nostrils. The leader was now sniffing and making quite a noise doing so.

"Hold your beards, brothers, some things are here that shouldn't be!'

All the miners then began to sniff so loudly that they reminded the children of vacuum cleaners. Esti and the children took to their heels and raced up the tunnel, but it was too late.

"Smell them out!" shouted the leader, and the miners gave chase, throwing themselves along the ground so they could grab the intruders' legs. Esti and Tom were caught first and held down despite their frantic struggles. Mackenzie and Rory charged back but could do nothing against so many. It was hopeless.

"What have we here?" said the leader, squinting with curiosity. "You're from up on the top, aren't you? Are you travelling players?" he asked hopefully. "Do you tell jokes?"

"Well, yes we do," said Rory boldly. "Knock knock!"

"Who's there?" responded their captor, eager to play.

"Ivan."

"Ivan who?"

"Ivan idea. You let us go."

The punch line was greeted by a shout of laughter.

"That was a good one. What a piece of luck. You are just what we need at the feast. Look what I've found for us," shouted the leader, though all his brothers were within inches of his face. "Entertainment. You four are herewith invited to our celebrations tonight, and what is more, you are the stars."

"We are very grateful," said Tom, "for the opportunity to entertain you all. But our schedule does not permit—I mean, can we do it another time?"

"Oh, no. Certainly not. Big gathering at headquarters tonight for all the brothers. You don't want to miss it, do you?"

He looked absolutely shocked at the idea.

"No, we wouldn't," added Mackenzie hastily.

"Big Chief gets elected tonight. He always gets elected on Fridays. He will be pleased. He likes a joke, and it stops him getting in a bad mood. Come on and I'll introduce you all!"

The children and Esti all agreed with a nod. After all, what else could they do?

"We are the Coblynau," the leader of the group replied airily. "I'm Mogun, and this is Mogette, and there's Mogmore over there, that little one is Mogless, and that one there is . . ."

"Mogger?" suggested Mackenzie.

Mogun looked at her astounded. "No, he's doing cooking today. Did you meet him before?"

"I might have, but I'm not sure."

"Well, no time to chat! Hurry up!" cried Mogun. "Must get to the feast."

So the three children and Esti were jostled along the path, which suddenly sloped downwards. The air became hotter and dry as sandpaper. No sign of roots now, for they were too deep underground. It was also much darker. Sometimes they had to go sideways, as the tunnel became narrow, then it sloped so low that they travelled on hands and knees. The Coblynau forgot to tell them to mind their heads, forgetting their entertainment were much taller than they were, and Rory and Mackenzie both bumped theirs.

"All right back there?" shouted Mogun every now and then.

Suddenly the tunnel opened up into an enormous cavern, with a roof supported by stalagmites as thick and tall as trees. The Coblynau sat along rows of trestle tables with sad, solemn faces and talked in low voices. Water dripped from the ceiling in a rhythm that sounded like a gentle drumbeat. Lanterns sat on the rock shelves and cast enormous shadows of the Coblynau hordes onto the cavern walls.

There was a sudden lull in the conversation, followed by the sound of many vacuum cleaners as the Coblynau tried to identify the source of the new smells. The four were led to the front of the hall and invited to sit on short, damp stalagmites. Mogun walked up to another Coblynau, larger and with an even bushier beard than all the rest, obviously Big Chief, and excitedly pointed to Esti and the children. Then, when all the vacuums stopped, Mogun faced his audience, cleared his throat, and began the introductions.

"Tonight we elect our Big Chief, Mogalong! And, dear Coblynau, we have a treat tonight to go with our feast. We were a-working hard today on the east seam, and what do we find but this here travelling circus! They have come all the way from the top just to entertain us with jokes, so I want you to give a warm welcome to the entertainment!"

The cavern nearly caved in, the applause was so thunderous. Then every Coblynau turned toward the front of the hall and waited expectantly.

"What are we supposed to do?" cried Tom, in a horrified whisper.

"Just stand up here and tell jokes, I think," said his sister.

"Please do not ask me," begged Esti. "All my jokes are hundreds of years old, and even the Coblynau will have heard them."

"Somebody's got to do something. Look, I can start." Rory stood up on his stalagmite.

"Knock, knock."

"Who's there?" replied a chorus of Coblynau.

"Boo!"

"Boo Who?"

"Don't cry. It's only a joke."

Tom could not believe his eyes. The little men laughed so hard they fell off their benches backwards. "That's a good one," they gasped and banged on the tables.

"I've got one." Mackenzie stood up. If that's all it took, she could do it!

"Knock knock."

"Who's there?"

"Lettuce."

"Lettuce who?"

"Let us go back to where we came from. Please!"

Some Coblynau had to lie on the floor and hold their stomachs because they were laughing so much. The cavern echoed with their snortings and chortlings.

"I think we're a hit! I never knew we were that funny."

"My turn," said Tom.

"I don't know if we should. They might burst if they laugh any more," said Mackenzie.

Mog started a slow handclap and shouted, "Mogby and you Mogter, join in. Moggie, come on!" Soon the whole cavern was clapping for more.

"Well, can't stop now," answered Tom.

"What does diamond become when it's placed in water?"

There was much scratching of heads. "Don't know that one Mog. Do you?"

"Wet!" shouted Rory.

"What happens to you when you spend too much time in a tunnel?"

"You go round the bend."

The Coblynau were completely out of control, but then the laughter died down abruptly, as if a switch had been thrown. The kitchen staff arrived carrying hot, steaming platters. Mealtime was obviously serious business, for the now very sober Coblynau tucked huge white napkins around their necks and grabbed knives and forks. Unfortunately, many dishes never reached the diners and many a *Crash! Bang! Clash! Bang!* was heard, followed by "Sorry there, Mogan." "Oops! Excuse me, Mogter." "A*hhhhh!* Was that your head, Mogly?"

Huge dishes of burnished tin were placed on long tables, dishes that looked more like troughs. First a brown steaming liquid was tipped into each. The helpings were enormous. Soon the cavern was filled with the smacking of a hundred little lips.

The children and Esti were soon served. Rory stirred his serving. "You know what this looks like?"

"Mud?" guessed Tom.

"We'll have to drink it, or we'll offend them." Mackenzie was anxious not to upset their hosts.

"Okay! Okay!" Rory took a sip. "Hey, it's good! It's warm, very rooty and sweet."

"Are you playing trick on me?" asked Tom suspiciously.

"Try it yourself."

Rory was proved right, and they all drank it as fast as the Coblynau.

The next course was soon on the table. The Coblynau did not believe in sitting around being polite. On the plate were diamonds the size of potatoes and little emeralds the size of peas. Nestling in among them were slices of gold, cut very thin. The plate steamed.

"You eat precious stones?" Tom asked Chief Mog.

"Not raw! We boil them first," he said in a huff. "For 99 minutes. But they might be a bit hard for your tastes. How long do you usually boil yours?"

"About the same," interrupted Rory to avoid Tom going into a long explanation.

The Coblynau had given up any pretense of table manners and were now pushing in their food with both hands. There were slurpings and belchings and chomping and sloshing noises throughout the cavern. Food was flying over the tables and landing on the floor.

"It must be good," thought Mackenzie, "judging by the way they are gobbling it up." So she ate a forkful of diamonds. They were as cool as spearmint and as crunchy as red apples. Her mouth tingled with the flavour. She tried the emeralds. They were hard, so she sucked them like gob-stoppers. As they got smaller and smaller, they tasted sweet and sour by turns. Then she bit into the slice of gold. It dripped with juice, like a ripe peach, but it was not at all sweet. In seconds her mouth felt like it was on fire. She quickly sucked on a diamond to take the burning away. "Don't try the gold," she wheezed out between hot breaths. "I hope as long as I live, I'll never taste anything as hot and spicy as gold."

For dessert they were served red jelly piled high in silver goblets. It wobbled as it was set down.

"It's red ruby jelly," announced Mog, "so cool and sweet it will just slide down your throat."

"It's delicious." Mackenzie gobbled it up like a Coblynau.

"We make the juice ourselves," boasted the Chief Mogalong. "We take off our socks and boots and squash the ruby berries with our feet. Takes ages, and then we leave it a few years to set."

"I think I'm full now," said Mackenzie.

To finish the meal, the Coblynau ate the silver goblets as if they were ice cream cones.

Now the feast was done, a cry rang out, "We want to dance!" The next minute every Coblynau was strapping little bells onto his knees and tying scarves around his neck as a flute and a drum began to play. With a-hurrying and a-scurrying, the little men moved the trestle tables, gathered in a big circle, and began to dance. The bells tinkled as they stomped and hopped, first on one leg and then on the other. There were many collisions and slippings and slidings on the food that had been dropped. The drum beat faster, and the big feet banged up and down as they whirled and spun.

"Our chance to get away." Esti was relieved. He nodded towards the mouth of the cavern. "We just have to make our way across to the entrance." They got up casually and strolled towards the exit. One or two Coblynaus were still sitting at the tables, perhaps too old to dance now.

"Greetings Mogton! Fine feast today," called out Tom politely, hoping not to arouse suspicion.

The old Coblynau nodded back.

It was very hot in the cavern from all the dancing, and the Coblynau stank with sweat. The children and Esti were very close to escape now, except that the entrance was blocked by a group of dancers. Mackenzie laughed and announced, "I'd love to dance! It looks so fun."

"I don't think you should," advised Esti. "Faerie music is very . . ."

Mackenzie ignored him. A Coblynau came up to her, bowed low, and said, "May I have the pleasure of this dance?"

Before she could reply, another Coblynau shoved the first aside. "No, she's dancing with me!"

"No, me!" shouted a third, and before she knew it, Mackenzie was swept away into the throng with each of the little men swinging her around in turn.

She was taller than the Coblynau, so Esti and the boys knew where she was. They could see her head bobbing up and down as she danced. Mackenzie laughed. It was such fun. She soon skipped as fast as her dance partners. The drum beat faster and faster, and more Coblynau came to take a turn to spin her. She was hotter and hotter and almost out of breath, but try as she might, she could not slow down. Her feet moved faster now, as though they had a mind of their own. As she flew past Esti, he grabbed her hand.

"Come on! We're not supposed to be enjoying ourselves dancing." Mackenzie bobbed up and down as he spoke. "Will you stand still?"

It was too late. He was talking to the back of her head as she gyrated back into the dance.

Tom and Rory made it to the cavern entrance.

"What is she doing?" asked Tom. "Let's get out of here. Can't we make her stop?" He shoved his way into the throng, but the crowd jostled him away. He could hear Mackenzie shouting to him, "I can't stop! Even if I wanted to. But I don't. I don't ever, ever want to stop!"

Esti and the boys formed a flying wedge and pushed through the dancers to pull her out, but she danced so quickly they could not catch her. Her face was bright red with exertion, and she panted so hard Esti wondered why she did not collapse. He panicked. "There's something very wrong!"

"Didn't the echo tell us not to dance?" Tom remembered.

"It's the music," Esti sobbed. "She's enchanted, and she'll dance to her death."

"What's the antidote? There must be one!" Tom was terrified.

"I'll make them stop!" Rory clenched his fists around the hilt of his sword.

"No, Rory! Wait." Tom closed his eyes. He must remember. He was sure there was something. A little rhyme came to his mind, something he had read in a folklore book.

Turn the clothes—it's a charm—
Inside out will keep from harm.

"Come on! We have to catch her!" Tom instructed. All three of them lunged at Mackenzie as she came by. Luckily, she slipped on a huge squashed diamond that some Coblynau had thrown on the floor, and she slipped into their arms. She danced up and down as Esti had hold of her left arm, Rory her right.

"Take her sweater off!" said Tom. "Just do it!" he insisted, noticing Rory had opened his mouth to protest.

"So hot." Mackenzie puffed and panted, and it was a great effort for her to speak. Esti pulled off one sleeve, Rory the other, still holding her. Tom pulled it over her head and off. Then he put her head through the neck hole, the sweater inside out. "Put it back on," he shouted above the noise that was getting louder.

"Too hot," moaned Mackenzie.

"Too bad," answered Tom.

They forced her arms through the sleeves.

The minute she was dressed in her inside-out sweater there was an ear-shattering shriek from the Coblynau. The music stopped, and the children and Esti were alone in the cavern. The Coblynau were gone, but the walls were covered with lumps and bumps that had not been there before.

"What camouflage!" Rory said in admiration. "What happened?"

Mackenzie's face was soaked with perspiration and her legs trembled with exhaustion. "Why couldn't I stop?" she whispered.

"Faerie music is not for mortal folk," Esti told her. "The spell you were under would have made you dance your life away."

Mackenzie hid her face in Rory's shoulder. "How did you make it stop?" she sobbed.

"Tom did it," explained Rory. "He's very smart."

Tom explained. "I just remembered that if you have your clothes on inside out, it's supposed to be a protection against the faeries." He smiled across at Rory.

Mackenzie struggled to get her breath back to normal. She had not yet recovered her strength, but they could not wait any longer.

"Let's get out of this place," she said, "while we still have the chance."

CHAPTER SEVEN
FIRE AND WATER

Madoc carefully led Vivienne out of the wood of Broceliand. They sat by the waterfall at Witch's Cauldron, where she slowly recovered her sight and hearing. Though she made progress, she was still quite deaf, and things in the distance were out of focus. This did not, however, deter her from her plots and schemes. Like a wasp that has been swatted, she was more bad-tempered and more dangerous.

She sat with Madoc, giving him orders.

"I shall return to the wood of Broceliand now I am recovered. I shall go to the place where Merlin rests, a place that has not seen my face for centuries. There I shall wait with you, my knight. In time Esti and those three horrible children will come there, and when they do, I will destroy them." She pulled up a handful of buttercups and ripped them to shreds.

Madoc sighed, ready to pour his heart out to the one he loved. "My Lady," he murmured, "I adore you. If you could see how . . ."

"What cow? I don't see a cow," she interrupted irritably. "I am talking about important matters."

Madoc, his heart full of adoration, tried again. "If you could see that . . ."

"Cat? Where is the cat? I wish you would not mumble so!"

Madoc gave up, and they prepared to leave. Madoc grabbed Vivienne's sleeve in the nick of time as she stalked off towards the edge of the waterfall, mistaking it for the path into the wood.

The three children and Esti ran through the network of tunnels beneath the place where Madoc and Vivienne sat only moments before. On and on they went, often looking behind, but no one followed. All they heard was their own footsteps. Just faintly at first, they became aware of the sound of water. Soon it was so loud they could hardly hear each other speak. The air coming down the tunnel was fresh and damp with spray, and the light at the end was so bright it made their eyes ache. Across the entrance was a curtain of sparkling water. The tunnel rose up, out of the ground, and opened right behind the waterfall. They waited there while Rory went ahead to check how they could get out. He was soaking wet when he came back.

"There's just enough footholds for us to scramble out from behind this waterfall, and then we can get up the bank of the river. Be careful though. It's really slippery. Esti, you go first and help Mackenzie. Then Tom. I'll watch our backs. Hold tight and don't look down!"

One by one they stepped out onto a rock ledge and inched toward the muddy path that would take them to the embankment at the top. Despite his own good advice, Rory could not help looking down to see how high they were. Way below was a whirlpool. Its frothy white water churned and smashed into jagged rocks that poked up like teeth. The water was sucked and blown as if by a gigantic mouth. Rory felt dizzy, and without realising it, his fingers loosened their grip on the rock.

Tom, beside him, noticed right away. "Rory! Look up! Hold on, just another step, ok?"

Rory looked right through Tom as if he did not recognize him.

"I, I, I just found out I'm scared of heights," he stammered.

"It's okay, Rory. We can do it. Just one more step. And another."

When they reached dry land, Tom said nonchalantly, "It was just vertigo." For once Rory did not make any remarks about talking dictionaries.

"Hey! Come and look at this. Looks like we just missed those two," called Mackenzie. In the mud were two footprints. One set was of boots trailing the marks of spiky spurs. The other set of prints was much smaller.

"Do you think it's them?"

"Most likely it is. Vivienne will not give up," Esti sighed.

"And neither will we," Tom said stoutly.

They left the riverbank and entered deep woods. Esti seemed confident of the way they should go.

"Well I remember this way through the woods," he said. "How can I ever forget that place and the terror of that day Vivienne took Merlin from me?"

Night fell. The full moon shone brightly, giving them some light. Suddenly they heard fire crackling and saw flames between the tree trunks.

"Get down!" cried Rory, pulling them all into the bracken. They peered through the fronds and saw they had almost walked straight into Vivienne's encampment. The light they saw came from many torches held aloft by knights in black armour. Standing among them was Vivienne. They could clearly see her scarlet dress. Around her shoulders was a cloak of feathers shining white, tawny, and gold. Her hood was the head of an owl, its glassy eyes staring through the twilight. The beak hung dead and still between the eyes of the enchantress. Shadows played on her face and contorted her features into a gruesome mask. The metal helms of her knights glinted in the flames.

Mackenzie remembered the effect Vivienne had on Esti, and she held him tight. "Don't look at her," she pleaded. "You've got to stay safe." Luckily, the crackle of burning bracken and dead wood disguised the sound of her voice so Madoc, standing nearby, heard nothing.

"What's *she* doing here?" Rory was frustrated.

"This is where Merlin is," Esti said simply. "I suppose she knew from Madoc that we would come here eventually."

Rory looked ashamed. "Diversion," he said. "We need a diversion to get her out of the way."

"I can do that," whispered Esti. "You stay here and get Merlin out of the rock."

"How are we supposed to do that?" asked Mackenzie horrified.

"And what if she catches you?" added Rory, with a worried look.

Before they could stop him, Esti stood up and shouted out, "I am here, Mistress! Come and get me!"

He ran out on to the path so she could see him, then took off through the undergrowth.

Vivienne's screams rent the air. "After him! Catch him!" she ordered the knights. "Do not let him get away, or you will pay. I created you from mist, and to mist you shall return!" The lighted torches of the knights bobbed up and down in the distance, where they continued the chase. Vivienne stayed by the fire, expecting the imminent return of the knights with her prey.

"This plan is not working," moaned Mackenzie. "She is not budging."

"I'll go and challenge her," said Rory. He was about to show himself when

some of the knights returned.

"We've lost him," they explained, in terror-stricken voices. Vivienne pointed her finger in rage at the lot of them and spoke words the children could not understand. As she spoke, each knight turned into a glimmering mist that wafted away on the night breeze. All, that is, except one, who kept apologizing.

"Shut up, Madoc!" she yelled. "You are of no use either!"

"My Lady, thanks to my tender care, you have regained all sight and hearing. I expect some little thanks. A kiss, perhaps, or—marriage?"

In answer, Vivienne screamed and stamped her foot.

"Shut up! I suppose I will have to catch the little wretch myself! You can guard the rock while I do it," she commanded. "And if you are so mindless or cowardly as to let anyone approach, you will never enjoy human form again."

"My Lady," sighed Madoc. "As if I would fail to carry out your bidding!"

He tried to kiss her hand, but his lips brushed feathers. Vivienne had already slipped her arms into the wings of the cloak and pulled the head of the owl over her face. When her transformation was complete, she swooped like a shadow into the moonlit night.

Madoc stuck a large torch into the ground and settled himself down on a feathered cloak. He leaned back on the sheer granite rock overgrown with orange lichen. On it was the mark of a hand. The bored knight peered into the trees on either side, whistled and drummed his fingers. Occasionally, he got up and strode around. He practiced a few thrusts with his sword. He threw himself back on the grass. "Nothing to do, nowhere to go, nobody to have a nice fight with!" He heaved a sigh. He reached for a wineskin tucked into his breastplate and took several long swigs, burped, and sighed. He took a few more.

"What are we going to do?" Mackenzie cried in frustration. "We don't have much time before she finds Esti."

"You're right," said Tom, "judging by how fast owls can fly. We've got to get rid of him!"

"Wait here." Rory gathered up a few stones, put them in his pocket, and stealthily climbed the tree nearest to them. Tom made some night bird noises to disguise the rustles and cracking twigs. Once Rory was at the top of the tree, he threw a stone behind Madoc. The knight perked up his ears. "Action!" he muttered with a grin. "Stand and give yourself up!" he barked into the trees and stumbled a little. "Maybe I shouldn't have had that last swig," he thought. He unsheathed his sword.

Rory threw another stone.

"I'm coming in to get you if you do not show yourself, you lily white coward!" Madoc tripped but got up again, with difficulty. He ran into the woods.

Rory came down from the tree and scampered deeper into the wood, making as much noise as he could to lead Madoc on. Rory drew his sword.

"Tom!" Mackenzie whispered. "Now's our chance! But what do I do?"

Tom stared at his sister's neck. The moonlight shone directly on the stone, and he saw seven colours gathering around it like a rainbow mist. The seven colours arced out of the stone and red, orange, yellow, green, blue, indigo, and purple hit the rock where Merlin was trapped. Where the colours fell, the rock became like a steamed-up window. Tom saw the shadow of a figure transfixed in the rock. He yelped in fright. "He's in there! He really is!"

A bellow of rage rang out, and Madoc ran back out of the trees.

"Aha! Got you! Yield unto me, for I am Madoc, the raven of the forest! I will catch you, and then my Lady will most likely love me forever." Madoc ran at Tom and grabbed him.

"Get your hands off him," yelled Rory, chasing Madoc. He shoved Madoc hard from behind, and the knight toppled over. Madoc let go of Tom but struggled back to his feet.

"Come on then, let me see what you can do," challenged Madoc. He thrust his sword vaguely in the direction of Rory's neck. He could not quite make out which blurry shape was Rory and which was a tree. Everything was spinning around.

Rory wondered if Madoc was more dangerous drunk or sober. Luckily, Rory was not drunk this time. By moonlight, he could easily see the knight. Madoc and Rory closed in battle, and sword clanged against sword. Madoc struck left and right, and Rory parried.

The knight was slow and heavy in his black armour. Rory, in jeans, was nimble and light, but unable to disarm Madoc, who was bent on doing as much damage as he could. When he got the chance, Rory ran behind Madoc.

Madoc swerved around, not sure where Rory went, spotted him, and swung his sword low to try and cut his legs. Rory leapt then quickly ducked when Madoc went for his neck.

"You perform well, squire, though not as well as I," Madoc remarked breathlessly as the swords flashed back and forth through the trees. Rory dented Madoc's armour, but remained unharmed. He doubted he could keep up the pace for long.

"Get Merlin out of the rock!" Tom shook Mackenzie, who looked as though she was turned to stone herself. "Sing! Quick, while he's busy trying to kill Rory."

"I'm a rusty nail. I can't!"

"Then why did the lady give you a harp?"

Mackenzie held the harp of bone and hair in her hands. "That's right. The Singer has a harp. I am *not* a rusty nail!" she thought. She ran her fingers ran across the strings, and notes rang out clear and sweet. "I *can* do it," she whispered, 'because I have my gift from the lady.'

"Mackenzie, hurry up!"

Mackenzie took a deep breath and sang with the harp a song of joy and liberation. The stone around her neck grew warm as it caught the notes and reflected the song into the night. Mackenzie's song echoed over and over again. It became seven songs, all Mackenzie's voice, harmonizing into one rich melody.

"Stop that!" shouted Madoc, who suddenly realised what was afoot. He breathlessly charged back to his place before the rock and pointed his sword at Mackenzie. Mackenzie stood still and held her breath. All was silent and still.

Rory charged and slammed into Madoc, who flew head first into a clump of stinging nettles. Rory jumped on to the Knight's back and sat astride him as if he were a horse. Tom ran over and jammed the knight's visor hard over his head.

"I think you'll need a can opener to get out of this!" cried Tom.

Madoc struck Tom as he flailed, leaving Tom winded and unable to get up.

Rory stood over the knight, his sword held to Madoc's throat. Madoc could not move. Rory heard a crashing noise and looked up. Vivienne came into the glade, dragging Esti behind her.

"Look out! She's back!" he yelled.

In the moonlight, Mackenzie saw Esti's face, covered with blood.

"So it is you, you meddling girl. You have got my stone. You stole it, you thief! Give it back now!" screamed Vivienne. "Everyone knows that all the snake stones belong to me!"

Mackenzie put her hands over the stone. "This is mine," she said, "and you shall never have it."

"You know nothing! Snake stones from the head of an adder always belong to me. Truth to tell, I thought there were none left in any worlds. This must be the last." Vivienne stretched out her hand for the stone, waggling her fingers. Give it to me, you little wretch, or I shall rip it from your neck." Vivienne advanced, then suddenly pulled her grasping hand back and screamed. "The protection is strong!"

Mackenzie felt an electric current tingle and buzz between her and Vivienne, as though she was protected by an invisible shield.

"It is a power stone," moaned Vivienne. "See how it builds a wall against me."

Again Vivienne sprang at Mackenzie but got no closer. Her magic was not strong enough.

Vivienne's voice was icy with rage. "*Give it to me!*"

Mackenzie looked into Vivienne's eyes. They were white with only a pinprick of a black pupil in the centre. Mackenzie shivered but stood her ground.

"You don't want anything to happen to your knight do you?" cried Rory thinking to bargain with her. Vivienne barely glanced over at him.

"That so-called knight is utterly useless! Why do I have to depend on oafs and idiots?"

"Forgive me, my Lady. I adore you!" Madoc's voice was very muffled inside his visor.

"Get ye gone, raven!" screeched Vivienne. Madoc crumpled before their eyes, grew feathers, and flew like a dart into the darkness of the forest.

"I don't care what you do to us!" said Mackenzie. "We shall wake Merlin. I promise you."

"I will make you care, you stupid girl. Take a look at your little friend. I warned you to stay away from Esti. He is quite unharmed for now," remarked Vivienne. "But you will learn how I deal with those who displease me. I intend to be avenged on the whole pack of you!"

Vivienne stretched out her hands towards the trees and undulated her fingers. Flames leapt from their tips, spat out like fireworks, and ignited the grass. The fire ran across the ground like a long yellow snake, crackling as it encircled the glade. Black smoke billowed into the air, scorching Mackenzie's throat. Her eyes began to smart. Tom coughed. Rory ripped up some bracken and tried to beat the fire out, but in a short time that too caught fire, and he was helpless to do more.

"*Give me my stone!*" shouted Vivienne.

A flock of birds flew screeching out of the trees, crying out a warning.

Mackenzie felt the animals' terror in the air, which scared her even more. The fire moved closer until it surrounded them.

"Give her the stone!" cried Esti, struggling to get up, "Or else you will all perish."

"Just sing!" shouted Rory.

"Get away and save yourselves!" Esti pleaded.

"Do it, Mackenzie!" urged Tom. "It's our only hope."

Mackenzie wanted to, but she was afraid to move. The fire roared. Vivienne's laughter was almost as loud as the fire.

"Hand it over, you ingrate, or I will burn down the whole forest, if necessary. Pray, do not alarm yourselves. The fire will not harm me!"

At that moment Mackenzie had only one thought: her mother. Didn't Esti say that once they saved Merlin he might be able to help her? And what about Esti and her brothers? Did she really think Vivienne would send them all back home as if nothing happened?

Mackenzie held the harp tightly and began to sing again. The song grew into seven songs, ever louder and stronger. The seven songs swelled to drown out the roar of the fire. Vivienne put her hands over her ears.

"Stop!" she screeched in pain and fell flat on her face

The ground shook. Trees rocked, creaked, and moaned. Rory helped Tom up, and they both ran to Esti, half carrying him to the little island of unburned grass on which Mackenzie stood.

The rock had a thin crack running down the middle. That crack branched into a second, then another and another until the entire surface was a network of cracks. Even though the glade was a carpet of flame, encroaching on their tiny circle of unburned grass, Mackenzie played and sang, on and on.

With a clap like thunder, the rock split in two. From the ground beneath it gushed a spring. Its water flowed into the glade. It poured so fast the ground was boggy in moments. There was a hiss as the fire was extinguished, bit by bit. The glade filled with steam as water hit fire.

Vivienne leapt into the air and flung out her arms, and they turned into wings. As an owl, she swooped down and picked up a mouse in her claws, a mouse in the exact spot Esti had stood.

"She's got away and taken Esti!" Rory cried, standing up and slashing the air with his sword. It was too late.

The three of them, black with soot and with ash in their hair, were spent. Their distress was so great they were hardly aware of someone moving through the clouds of steam and smoke. A tall figure, a grey-cloaked man, leaned on a staff, coughed, and gasped for air. As he stretched out his arms, they heard a crackle of electricity and saw hazy blue sparks scatter from him, like drops of water.

He knelt down heavily on the scorched earth beside them, tears on his cheeks. His proud ashen face was stern and old, his eyes golden and catlike. His mane of hair, like his beard, was grey, shot red threads.

His breathing became more ragged. His life was slipping away.

CHAPTER EIGHT
THE STONE CIRCLE

"Now what do we do?" Mackenzie was frantic, but Tom was already taking the stopper out of the drinking horn and put it to Merlin's lips. The magician spluttered as the drops ran into his mouth. Soon, colour returned to his face and his breathing became regular and deeper. When he spoke, his voice was strong.

"I thank you for such a healing draught! But don't I recognize that horn from somewhere?"

"Yes, you probably do. I heard it was yours," Tom handed it to Merlin, a little embarrassed.

"No, it is yours now," said Merlin. "I know this was blessed by the lady of the directions and contains the healing draught." He looked at each of them in turn. "Tell me, who released me from my captivity? Can you be The Three?"

"No," answered Tom. "We're just three kids! And now Esti's gone."

"Vivienne took him. I couldn't stop her!" Rory tried to stay calm. "She nearly burnt us all to death. Now we're safe, but Esti's in her clutches again."

Merlin got to his feet and leaned heavily on his staff. "Esti will return. Do not distress yourselves. Pray, tell me your names."

"I'm Rory, and this is my brother, Tom, and my sister, Mackenzie."

"And how did you free me from the enchantment?"

Mackenzie showed him the stone and her harp. "This is how we did it, Sir," she told him.

"Ah, you have the Stone of Power, a snake stone!" His eyes gleamed. "In ancient times, snake stones belonged to wise women and were handed down from mother to daughter. Is that how it came to you, Mackenzie?"

"My mother gave it to me," Mackenzie answered quietly. Merlin looked into her eyes. She saw such kindness in him. Somehow she thought he knew about her mother. Suddenly she realized, if Esti knew something, then Merlin knew it too.

"You must go back to your world soon," he said suddenly. "But first, we must deal with the great enchantress, Vivienne."

Tom spoke up. "But, Sir, look, your staff is dead and you seem so—old. You don't know what she is like. She is crazy and can do just about anything!" He did not like to come out and say it, but he didn't think Merlin could stand up to Vivienne, especially if he was going to try and get Esti away from her.

"Some of my powers will return anon," Merlin promised, "though the final success of the quest does not rest with me. Vivienne will try to go back to your time with Esti. She must take my boy Esti, as much of her power comes from him. He is part of me. Vivienne thinks she is safe in your world, in your time. She likes to continue her evil ways unchallenged. But to get back to your world, she will have to go back the same way she left."

"What way is that?" asked Rory.

"Through the door on Bran's Hill, within the stone circle. She is probably going there now."

"Come on then. Let's go get her and rescue Esti!" urged Rory.

"And so we shall," answered Merlin. "Before the sun is up, Vivienne and I must be gone to the Islands in the West, through one of the doorways on Bran's Hill."

"And Esti," Mackenzie reminded him. "You forgot to say Esti."

"He will be there, but his journey is ended." Merlin said softly.

"I'm going to miss him," admitted Rory sadly, not really understanding.

"All must go home in the end."

"We are going home too," said Mackenzie. "Merlin, will you help my mother get well?"

Merlin smiled at her, and she looked deeply into his tawny yellow eyes. "It will be a gift from Esti. Although you do not understand it now, you will understand when the time comes.

They set off for Bran's Hill. It was just starting to get light as they climbed its slopes, covered with brown bracken and stubbly grass, shorn by grazing sheep. They could see across a grand panorama. The hills slept in the early morning mists, and they could follow the river as it wound through the valley. It spilled like a horse's tail over the rocks, forming the waterfall known as the Witch's Cauldron, where they had been such a short time ago.

They were glad to reach the stone circle at last. Like living beings, the stones seemed to welcome them. Most were at least twice the height of a man. Some stood as straight and true as they did the day they were erected. Others had been destroyed or had fallen down over the years and were covered with green moss and orange lichen. In the center of the circle was one long, flat stone, pitted and cracked with the weathering of millennia. This stone was illuminated by the first rays of the sun, which had just begun to rise between the two stones to the east.

Merlin pointed with his staff at the sun and spoke anxiously. "We must be gone before the sun rises above those two stones, or else the door to the west will be shut to us."

"I hope she hurries up," said Tom. "There's not much time then."

They wandered to the edge of the circle and looked down the slopes, but there was still no sign of Vivienne. Rory kept watching the skies, trying to spot an owl, in case Vivienne returned in that form with a mouse in her talons. The sun was now halfway up between the two stones.

"She must come," Merlin reassured them and himself. "It is her only way out of this time and place."

"Unless she has another of her special surprises in store for us," added Rory. Tom felt his heart sink.

Suddenly Rory shouted and pointed down into the valley below where he saw a woman riding a black horse. As she climbed the hill, he was sure it was Vivienne. Her red dress blazed like a wound in the early morning light. It looked as though a bundle of black rags was tied to the saddle behind her, but soon they saw it was Esti.

Vivienne saw the children and Merlin himself silhouetted against the sky and shook her fist. She then turned her horse as if to flee back down the hillside. Merlin clenched his staff so the knuckles showed white. "I never thought to see her ride away in fear," he said.

Suddenly, changing her mind perhaps, Vivienne kicked her horse into a gallop and rode up the hill towards them.

"Watch it! She's thinks she can take us on and win," murmured Mackenzie. "But we know her pretty well by now."

"Tom, Rory, stand by the centre stone with Mackenzie. Quickly!" ordered Merlin. "Mackenzie's stone has shown you already how it can protect you from Vivienne."

"No, I'll stand just here," answered Rory, reaching for his sword.

"No you don't!" ordered Merlin. "That sword has no power against magic!"

Rory relented, and the three of them did as they were bid. "All are safe here," promised Merlin. "Have no fear." With his staff, Merlin drew a circle of white light around them all.

Vivienne entered the stone circle and took in the sight of the three children and Merlin in the protected centre. She sneered and rode right up to the ring of white light, dismounted, and pulled Esti from the horse. In his weakened state he would have collapsed into a heap on the ground had not Merlin run forward, out of the protected place, and caught Esti in his arms. He put him down gently on the grass.

"My boy," said the old wizard as tears ran down his cheeks. "At last!"

"Oh, Father! You are free!" cried Esti. "Why did you ever leave me! I have been in deep sorrow such long ages!" Esti clung to Merlin as though to never let him go. "No one loved me! I was so sad, Father. My heart was breaking."

Mackenzie saw the rope marks and fresh cuts on Esti on top of the old bruises Vivienne had given him.

Merlin held Esti tightly. "Yes, yes, my own dear boy. I missed you so much. I am full of sadness, and I am so sorry I left you alone to suffer so. I wish it had never been so. It was my foolishness, my madness that caused it all. Please forgive me, my boy."

"I wish we could be together again. Just like we used to be! We were so happy." Esti's voice was hopeful, his eyes pleading.

"Everything ends in this world, Esti." Merlin's voice was low. "Those times will never come again. It is time for you to be free, to go to the beautiful meadows of Mag Mell. You know we spoke of such end times long ago. There you will never know suffering again, only peace."

"This is so touching!" rang out Vivienne's harsh voice. "I have heard enough! Stop making such a fuss over him! He is nothing. The girl with the stone managed to crack that rock. So what! It won't take me long to put you back there, I swear! And as for Esti, he is my boy now and always will be!"

"Accept what is to be. This is the end for you and for me, Vivienne. Esti will not be anyone's boy ever again."

"What is going to happen?" cried Mackenzie, afraid now. "Is Esti going to die!"

"Esti is thought, and he will live forever," Merlin replied, not taking his eyes from Esti's. "His form will leave him, and still he will live, only not in your world." Merlin smoothed Esti's hair as Esti became calm and his tears dried.

"Thank you, Father," he whispered. "You show me in my mind the rest of my journey. I know I am part of you, always and forever."

"My boy, so brave and true!" Merlin helped Esti to stand up so he could speak to The Three. "Mackenzie, Tom, Rory, I may not tarry nor may I bide and now I leave forever. Mackenzie, do not fail me. By the power of song and stone, my torment is at an end. Not just for me, but all here will be free and healed. The prophecy is fulfilled and darkness will be driven back."

Vivienne screamed. "I curse you all! I will destroy you! I will lay waste this land! I will bring despair! None of you will ever leave this place! I swear it!"

"Lady Vivienne. After so long a separation, I behold you again, and you have changed not one whit," Merlin answered.

"'Tis true. My loveliness shines as bright as ever," she said sweetly, masking the rage in her eyes. "Who would guess my age?" She laughed to herself. "Why, in truth, do you care so much about Esti when I am near?" She tossed her long, shimmering hair. "I suppose you still love me, Merlin? Incarceration has not dimmed that conflagration of love and affection you once had for me?" Her words may have sounded like a question, but her tone of voice suggested she thought she could easily captivate Merlin one more time. She came close to him and looked deep into his eyes, then pulled away in disappointment.

"Oh, I see. You are cured of your mad love for me."

"I am myself again," he replied.

Her face was grim, but only for a moment. Then she smiled slowly. "Ah, but you cannot be yourself again, can you? The greater part of your magic is mine and mine alone! You are nothing. I have all because I still have Esti. You have neither means nor ways to take him from me," she laughed shrilly.

Merlin lifted his staff high in his right hand. It was green with life and had sprouted thick, new leaves.

"Not all my magic." He cried aloud, "Behold my staff! My powers return."

"So you intend to challenge me?" She bent over double, she was laughing so hard. "You stupid old man," she howled.

"I have not come to challenge you, only to take you with me," said Merlin. "You must bid farewell to the world of The Three and leave for the Islands in the West. We go now. Our leaving is long overdue."

"I am not going anywhere. I like it where I am. There is so much for me to do."

"I know the things you like to do. Is their world not sad enough, without your hands making more and more trouble?"

"No one can stop me. Least of all you! Get thee hence, old man! Leave me alone!"

She pulled her hands together as though she held a ball between them. She was fashioning a sphere of grey light. As it formed, the scent of rot grew pungent in the air. When she was satisfied, she threw the light up into the air where it fragmented into a cloud of buzzing, stinging insects that headed straight for Merlin. The magician waved his staff, and a silver net appeared and enclosed the swarm. The insects melted into the air.

"Very clever," Vivienne hissed. "But I was not trying so very hard. It was just a taste of what I can and will do if you do not leave me alone!"

"You cannot prevent this. It is our destiny. We leave together."

"Who will make me?"

"The Three." He pointed to Mackenzie, Tom, and Rory.

"Are you serious, Merlin?" Vivienne laughed. "Your mind was certainly addled in your imprisonment. They are nothing more than feeble children."

"Perhaps you do not see them well. I must remove the veils that blind you."

He hit the ground three times with his staff. White light poured from the tip and surrounded the children like a cloud. When it lifted, Rory stood radiant in the light of the sun. In his hand he held the sword that glinted silver. Beside him stood Mackenzie, the stone ablaze on the chain around her neck. On her arm was her harp. Next to her was Tom. His hands grasped the horn of the elixir of knowledge for those whose mind is strong enough to taste the draught.

"Behold the Warrior, the Singer, and the Sage. And you, Vivienne, did not even know them! How can you be such a great enchantress when you, oh mighty sorceress, failed to recognize The Three?"

Vivienne went white and stiff as stone. She shook with rage. Something within in her dimmed. "I would have crushed their bones that first day!" Her anger diminished as she remembered something. "But as long as I have Esti, you can do nothing against my will. As long as he exists, you are incomplete."

"That will be remedied now, Vivienne."

Merlin turned to the Warrior, the Sage, and the Singer. "Remember the words of the prophecy," he said. "You have freed the mage, and now it is time to free the thought. Mackenzie, you must unmake Esti's form and give him his freedom, as you gave me mine. He wishes to bid farewell to you, for it is time."

Esti held their hands, each in turn. "Farewell, brave Rory. Those were very noble battles you fought on this quest against the griffin and Madoc, the Raven of Battle."

Rory looked ashamed. "I'm remembering some of the other stuff I did," he muttered.

"You are yourself now. Henceforth, choose your battles wisely."

Rory looked at his feet and smiled.

"Farewell, wise Tom. I'll never forget how you knew the griffin's name in Greek, how you remembered the charm in the Coblynau cave, or how you saved Rory above the waterfall." Tom looked embarrassed, but he smiled.

"Farewell, gentle Mackenzie, whose courage was great enough to pass the griffin and to guess his name, whose compassion was so strong that you risked everything to help a poor, simple thought like me. You sang the song and woke Merlin, and now you shall free me!"

He turned to all of them. "All your deeds were mighty, and even more than this," laughed Esti, "you tell such wonderful knock-knock jokes!"

"Nothing ever can stay the same," explained Merlin to the children. "You care about my boy, and I thank you for that. All three of you freed Esti. His work is done. Mackenzie, now stand upon the centre stone, for it is the place of great power."

Mackenzie did so and, with tear-stained face, ran her fingers over the strings of the harp. This time she knew what she had to do, and deep inside she knew she could do it. Notes from the harp rang out like liquid air. She joined the notes with her sweet voice, and as she did, the song penetrated the stone around her neck and radiated out of it, not as seven songs this time, but as seven colours.

The first was a fiery light as red as blood. It flared towards Esti, and when it touched him he glowed and red poured out of him. As the red touched all their minds, they felt brave and strong.

Mackenzie sang, and orange, bright as a flame, surrounded Esti and took orange light from him. It gave them power and confidence before it faded.

Mackenzie sang on, and yellow streamed from the stone to Esti, bringing deep joy to their minds. As yellow left him, Esti became insubstantial, like a ghost.

Mackenzie's voice trembled and almost broke as she saw Esti becoming less and less solid. Yet she sang again, and the song brought forth a green light, a wispy fog, that brought healing and love into the circle. Even Vivienne seemed to respond to the colour for a moment, for her face looked softer, kinder. But this time, some of the green light pulsated and entered the stone around Mackenzie's neck and did not dissipate. Now Esti was mere mist that shifted in the breeze like a column of smoke.

Next came blue, a light that brought peace. Mackenzie held back her tears as blue left Esti, and he no longer had any semblance of human form.

Finally, indigo poured forth, and Esti was gone. A deep, rich violet cloud filled the circle and clouded in the place where Esti had been. The sun was now deep orange, staining the clouds, fully risen between the stones. Merlin stood before them surrounded by a rainbow of radiant light.

"Blessings on you all! Truly you are The Three. The quest is complete, and it is time to go home. May joy be with you. Farewell, Singer, Warrior, and Sage. Esti has given you the green light of healing in your stone, Mackenzie. All three must now send it to the one you love."

Merlin took the reins of the horse. It reared up as it felt the magician on its back. Merlin kicked his heels, and the horse galloped at full tilt toward Vivienne, who stood afraid and helpless. Merlin leaned over in the saddle and gathered her, unprotesting, into his arms. The horse raced towards Mackenzie, who was still standing on the stone slab in the center of the circle, then soared high into the air above her. Horse and riders were suspended in the air for a moment, and, with a flash of lightning, they disappeared.

"Esti's gone. He's left us nothing but his memory." The boys stared at each other, bewildered. Mackenzie took charge and, with trembling fingers, removed her necklace. "More than memory," she stated. "Didn't you see? The green light, the healing light, came from Esti into my stone!"

"The healing!" cried Tom, catching on. "He left healing green for Mother! Okay. I think we all should put our hands around the stone and imagine sending this healing to Mother. I'm sure that's what we're meant to do. At least I think that's what Merlin meant. And he did make us a promise."

Mackenzie put the stone in the palm of her hands, and both boys cradled her hands in theirs. They felt heat coming from the stone, soothing and full of love. Each thought very hard about their mother. They kept their hands like that until Mackenzie noticed, "The stone feels like a piece of ice! I'm sure that means the healing has gone to her. The stone is empty."

"She is going to get better! I really, really believe it!" said Tom.

"I want to believe it," said Rory.

"Are you ready?" said Mackenzie. "Let's go home."

Mackenzie spun the crystal as before into a kaleidoscope of colours that dazzled their senses. It was as if every colour in the world had been sucked into the spinning crystal and they were living for the moment inside a black-and-white photograph. They felt giddy, their vision blurred, and they lost the sense of where they were. Then they found themselves curled up among the branches of the lightning-struck tree. All was as before, except Esti was not there and Mackenzie still carried the harp, Tom the horn, and Rory the sword.

The sun was shining as if it were noon, as if no time had passed since they left with Esti. They looked at their gifts.

"Let's leave them here, in the tree, just in case. We might need them again!"

They placed the gifts among the branches and leaves. The harp, the sword, and the horn disappeared like objects hidden in a picture. Mackenzie thought if she squinted just a little, she could make out their outlines.

"I think everything is really safe here!" announced Rory.

"I should think so. I can't see a thing," replied his brother. Rory laughed, but Mackenzie noticed it was with Tom, not at him.

They hurried back to Aunt Maer's, raced through the front door, forgetting about wet feet and mud. Their aunt was just hanging up the phone. She looked at them in astonishment.

"That was good timing!" she said. "You've hardly been gone five minutes!"

"What's happened?"

"Have you heard from Dad?"

"Was that him?"

"Shhh. I can't think with you all shouting like that. Yes, I just got a phone call from Toronto. It was your father. He wants you to come home. Your mother woke up from the coma!" Aunt Maer's smile was so big her face lit up. "Your mother is awake. She is going to get better! You'd better start packing. It's time to go home."

Printed in Canada